SHADOW THIEF: JAILBREAK
BY
DAVID LOWRIE

TEXT COPYRIGHT © 2020 BY DAVID LOWRIE
ART COPYRIGHT © 2020 BY DAVID LOWRIE

LABYRINTHS OF LAEVENI
BY
DAVID LOWRIE

TEXT COPYRIGHT © 2020 BY DAVID LOWRIE
ART COPYRIGHT © 2020 BY DAVID LOWRIE

10 9 8 7 6 5 4 3
THIRD PRINTING, 2020

ISBN 9-798618004930

BLACK DOG GAMEBOOKS

BLACKDOGGAMEBOOKS@GMAIL.COM

# Shadow Thief

## Book one:

# Jailbreak

### Words and pictures

### By

### David Lowrie

Front cover by Michael Sheppard

# BLACK DOG GAMEBOOKS

# Acknowledgements

## Rob Hatton

## James Spearing

Thanks to both of you for helping by play testing this book and looking for any gremlins.

Thanks also to the members of the Facebook **Gamebook Authors Guild** for their advice, generosity and support. Having an on-line community for me as a first time writer has been a great experience. Thanks in particular to:

Dane Barrett

Victoria Hancox

Sam Isaacson

Mark Lain

Dave Lewis

Adam Mitchell

Sean Danger Monaghan

Martin Noutch

Adam Pestridge

James Schannep

Troy Anthony Schermer

Richie Aspen Stevens

And, finally thanks to my family for supporting me, as I endlessly doodle, draw, print, type, read, cross-out, swear and stick pieces of A4 paper together (should've used A3)

# Playing a gamebook

The chances are that if you have bought this book, then you will probably know what a gamebook is. If so, then please feel free to move on straight away to the next section.

If by some chance you haven't played a gamebook before, then it's basically interactive fiction. Most books are sequential. You start at page 1 and read page 2, 3 etc. until you get to the final page and the end and each time you read it, the book is the same and the story is the same.

In a gamebook, however, you make choices which indicate which way the story goes. The book is divided up into numbered sections. You start at section **1**. You read the text, and you are given the option of, for example, turning left, or turning right.

If you turn left you will be told to turn to a new section, let's say **142**. If you decide to turn right, then you are told to go to section **34**. Therefore, the choices you make determine which route you take through the book. I would say that you are the hero in your own story, but let's see, shall we?

As well as that, you also create a character, with different attributes. In this book there are things like fighting skill, endurance and agility. Your fighting skill helps you when you meet beings you may have to fight. Your endurance is how healthy or close to death you are, as you can easily die in this book - probably many times in many different but equally gruesome ways. If your endurance gets to zero, then unless told otherwise, you are dead and your adventure will end. This means you will have to start the book again – and maybe try a different route, or just be luckier.

Things like fights and tests are determined by rolling dice and adding them to different attributes. For this book you will need 2 6 sided dice (called d6).  So if you are told to roll 2d6 – you roll two six sided dice and add the numbers together. If you are told to roll 1d6 – roll 1 6 sided die.

As well as dice, you will also need a pencil (not a pen!), a rubber and paper. To keep track of your attributes, which will change over time, there is an adventure sheet in this book which you can write on, or ideally photocopy so you can use them again and again.

I would also recommend using blank paper to draw a map, or a route through the book, as there may be times when the path is not clear and mapping where you have already been will help you immensely.

Of course, this being your gamebook now (as hopefully you have bought it from me) then you can ignore the dice rolling etc., and just read it and try to find your way through without worrying about dying. It's entirely up to you.

So, whichever way you choose, then I hope you enjoy your time playing this book. This is my first published gamebook, and so there may be errors, typos or mistakes. If you do find any then please let me know by joining and commenting on my Facebook page:

**THE HELLSCAPE GAMEBOOK SERIES**

Or via:
Twitter:        **Black_dog_gamesbooks @ BGamebooks**
Instagram**:**  **blackdoggamebooks**
Email:         **blackdoggamebooks@gmail.com**

Any feedback would be much appreciated. If you get stuck, drop me a line and I will give you a hand (if you deserve it!).

The Facebook page will also keep you informed of upcoming gamebooks that I am in the process of writing.

# Your character's statistics

Throughout your adventure you have a series of stats that will determine how good you are at fighting, how fortunate you are, how long you can keep going for and how quick you are. Each of these need to be generated by rolling dice and recording them on the Adventure sheet in the book. These attributes will change over time – normally for the worst!

# Fighting Skill

Roll 1d6 and add 6. This is mainly used in combat. It is how proficient you are with arms and in hand to hand combat. There may be weapons or other items that will enhance (or decrease) your **FIGHTING SKILL (FS)**. Your **FIGHTING SKILL,** can go above its original value with some additions.

# Agility

Roll 1d6 and add 6. **AGILITY** is useful in lots of ways. In combat it helps you defend against attacks. In pursuits, or other times, then it can help you escape from enemies. It can also help you dodge traps due to your speed of movement. It can never exceed its original value, unless you are told otherwise.

# Endurance

This is the ability of your human form to carry on and take wounds. To find out your endurance, roll 2d6 and add 12. If your **ENDURANCE** gets to 0 during a game, your physical form is dead, and your adventure is (most likely) over. You will have to start the book again.

# Fitness

To find out your **FITNESS**, roll 1d6 and add 6 to the score. Fitness is your ability to keep on running, moving or fighting despite your all too human body getting tired. If you are in a fight, the longer it goes on, then the more fitness has to do with it – as you get tired and so are less able to attack and defend effectively. Fitness will go down by a point after each round of a fight or pursuit. However, this is only temporary, and it will return back to full levels by one point each subsequent paragraph. So if you go into a second fight soon after a first, you will be less able to fight.

# Intelligence

This is the ability to think and reason. The higher your **INTELLIGENCE**, the more likely that you may be able to escape traps, outwit enemies and work out the logical puzzles. Roll 1d6 and add 6.

# Fortune

This is the most random of characteristics. Sometimes pure chance will decide your fate. Some items you find may help (or hinder) your fortune so be careful when deciding what you want to take with you. Each time you test your fortune, subtract one from your **FORTUNE** score if you fail – as luck is fickle, and good fortune does not last. To find out your initial fortune, roll 1d6 and add 6.

# Shadow Thief: Jailbreak

## Adventure Sheet

| | | |
|---|---|---|
| Fighting Skill | 1d6 + 6 | |
| Agility | 1d6 + 6 | |
| Fitness | 1d6 + 6 | |
| Intelligence | 1d6 + 6 | |
| Fortune | 1d6 + 6 | If you fail a FORTUNE roll, reduce your fortune by 1 |
| Endurance | 2d6 + 12 | |

| Skills (pick 5) | Items | Notes |
|---|---|---|
| | | |

# Combat

| OPPONENT | FS | END |
|----------|-----|-----|
| *Name* | | |

Shadow

| END | FS |
|-----|-----|
| | |

| OPPONENT | FS | END |
|----------|-----|-----|
| *Name* | | |

Shadow

| END | FS |
|-----|-----|
| | |

| OPPONENT | FS | END |
|----------|-----|-----|
| *Name* | | |

Shadow

| END | FS |
|-----|-----|
| | |

| OPPONENT | FS | END |
|----------|-----|-----|
| *Name* | | |

Shadow

| END | FS |
|-----|-----|
| | |

| OPPONENT | FS | END |
|----------|-----|-----|
| *Name* | | |

Shadow

| END | FS |
|-----|-----|
| | |

| OPPONENT | FS | END |
|----------|-----|-----|
| *Name* | | |

Shadow

| END | FS |
|-----|-----|
| | |

# Combat

| OPPONENT | FS | END | | | | Shadow | |
|----------|----|----|--|--|--|--------|--|
| *Name* | | | | | | END | FS |

| OPPONENT | FS | END | | | | Shadow | |
|----------|----|----|--|--|--|--------|--|
| *Name* | | | | | | END | FS |

| OPPONENT | FS | END | | | | Shadow | |
|----------|----|----|--|--|--|--------|--|
| *Name* | | | | | | END | FS |

| OPPONENT | FS | END | | | | Shadow | |
|----------|----|----|--|--|--|--------|--|
| *Name* | | | | | | END | FS |

| OPPONENT | FS | END | | | | Shadow | |
|----------|----|----|--|--|--|--------|--|
| *Name* | | | | | | END | FS |

| OPPONENT | FS | END | | | | Shadow | |
|----------|----|----|--|--|--|--------|--|
| *Name* | | | | | | END | FS |

# Making "Test your "rolls

There will be (possibly) many times when you are told to test an attribute. Unless told otherwise, the normal thing to do is roll 2d6 and compare this to the attribute you are testing.

If you roll less than or equal to your current score in that attribute, you pass. If you roll higher, you fail and have to face the consequences. The act of rolling 2d6 may be the difference between life and death!

For example, if you **TEST YOUR FORTUNE**, roll 2d6 and compare that to your current **FORTUNE** score. If it is less than or equal to your current score, then you pass.

# Combat

Combat is often avoidable, but sometimes inevitable. To get through this ordeal, there will be times when strength of arms or an iron fist are the only way you can proceed.

This type of combat is aimed at those who either haven't played many game books, or just want to have a quick play through. This is the same as a lot of game books, in that you and your enemy both have a **FIGHTING SKILL (FS)**.

You roll 2d6 for your character and add the result to your **FIGHTING SKILL**. Now roll 2d6 and add the resulting number to your opponents **FIGHTING SKILL**.

The one with the higher total has hurt the other and loses 2 **ENDURANCE** points. You continue until you or your opponent has 0 **ENDURANCE (END)** – and so is dead or defeated.

# Skills

It's been three years since you were indoctrinated into the Guild of Thieves. In that time your rise through the ranks has been nothing short of remarkable. Still just out of your teens, you have a reputation as being one of the best thieves in the illustrious 800-year history of the Guild. You have pulled off some of the most infamous heists and theft in recent guild history and are one of the Guild Masters most trusted lieutenants.

Due to your promise and proven abilities, you have been given additional training in the Skills of the Masters.

During this time, you have mastered 5 of the Skills of the Master Thief.

You have done in 3 years what most do in 10 years. Please choose 5 of these skills and write them on your adventure sheet. They are divided into physical and mental skills. You can choose as all physical, all mental, or a combination of both

Some may help you in this adventure, some may not but will do in further adventures. So choose wisely.

# Physical Skills

**Speed and Agility**: All thieves are agile and quick, but you have been given additional training to give you the agility of a trained gymnast. It also means that your body is subtle and limber, and you are able to often fall and land on your feet, or roll to reduce injury.

You are also able to move much faster than most people, both in reflexes and physical speed. This means you can often outrun opponents, or react quicker to allow you to get the first strike in.

**Move silently and hide in shadows**: Stealth is a vital part of a thief's skill set, and working predominantly after night you are at home in the shadows. You are able to easily slip into the shadows and seemingly disappear from view as if by magic.

Your training and clothing also allow you to move almost silently on most surfaces and to pass without leaving a trace – except in the most extreme conditions. Having lived mainly in the dark, you also have exceptional night vision. However, due to your overly sensitive vision, bright lights or environments can sometimes dazzle you.

**Lock picking**: One of the first things you were taught was to pick a lock. You are able to open all but the most complicated locks in a matter of moments, and also know how to jam a lock to make it un-openable – even to someone with a key.

You are also trained in the use of corrosive potions that can help to dissolve the largest and sturdiest locks or barricades. Your trusty lock picks are sewn into the soles of your soft leather boots. Do not lose them, as your ability without them is limited.

**Climbing**: You are just at home on the roof tops as you are on the streets. Having lived on these rooftops for several hours a day most nights since you were a child, you have become an expert in climbing onto roof tops and scaling almost vertical walls.

Sown into the sleeves of your clothes are also "cat's claws" that you can quickly put over your hands to give you extra grip. However, given the majority of this experience was gained in the town, you are less at home climbing in the wild – although you will still have an advantage over most others.

**Unarmed combat**: Fighting is not the greatest attribute of a thief, who would rather use stealth, guile and distraction. You also have little love for blood, preferring not to kill, not for moral reasons so much as the attention it draws.

However, at times you may be cornered and fighting is your only option. You have been trained in various martial arts that give you an advantage whilst fighting most unarmed foes. However, there are limitations, and this skill will be of little use against an experienced and armed opponent. So try to avoid fighting. Unless it's the final resort.

# Mental Skills

**Charm and guile**: As a thief, you may find yourself in a situation whereby the options are either to fight your way out, or talk your way out. Against armed guards fighting is unadvisable. However due to your promise, you have been given training in the manners and ways of courtiers, and educated to a much higher level than a common cut purse. This charm allows you to extricate yourself from many a perilous situation, and also the ability to con and persuade others to do what you want.

**"Sixth Sense"**: Your additional training in paying close attention to your environment has given you the ability to sense or know when something is not as it seems. This can be useful for a number of reasons. You can often tell when a person is lying, or not who they appear to be. Similarly, you can often sense when a situation is just "wrong", such as a potential trap – physical or mystical. This sixth sense has alone saved your life on 7 occasions. However, this ability is limited when moving fast or using your agility as the environment moves too quickly for even your enhanced senses.

**Chakra**: You have almost complete control over your sympathetic and parasympathetic nervous system. You can slow your breathing and pulse to appear almost dead, you can enter a trance to reduce your need for oxygen, food and water, and you can use the natural energies of your own body to speed up the healing of minor wounds and sprains. However, when you are using this ability, it negates all your other skills – and so make sure that you only use it when it's safe to do so – or you have no choice!

**Forbearance**: This may not seem like a skill, but many a thief has ended up dancing at the end of a gibbet due to alacrity. There is a well-known saying in the Guild that "A hasty thief is often a dead thief". Regular mental training has given you the strength of mind to ignore potentially dangerous impulses, and you think nothing of waiting for hour upon hour for the right moment to strike. You have also trained yourself to keep your body subtle and responsive during times of inactivity, to avoid stiffness and cramping. You can also, despite being exhausted, often resist the temptation to sleep.

**Divvy:** As a thief you handle a lot of valuables – mostly stolen! However, you must always be aware that there are a lot of fakes around. A combination of experience, education and training has given you the ability to spot a fake.

# Equipment

You start your nights work in your normal thief's outfit. You are wearing plain and unremarkable clothing in black and grey. All black looks suspicious whilst moving though the town. Your jerkin is of the softest and subtlest leather, and adds protection of a light suite of leather armour. A hood is hidden in the neck of the jerkin. Cat's claws are also sewn into the arms of the jerkin that can be used to aide climbing.

Your boots are also the softest leather, with added grip to the very soft soles to allow purchase when climbing whilst still allowing you to move with great stealth. Sewn into a false sole of your left boot is your set of lock picks. In the top of the right boot, there are a couple of small phials of corrosive potions.

You are armed only with a two long thin sharp stilettos, well-hidden in a scabbard along your back. They are perfectly balanced and can also be thrown. You also have a small length or wire with a hook, a 20m coil of lightweight slim rope, a collapsible bag for your loot, a handful of poisoned caltrops and 20 gold pieces.

You are carrying no provisions as you are not expecting a journey, but have some snacks to give you energy enough to give you a boost of 2 endurance points.

Tonight started just as practically every other night has done for the last three years – on the roof tops.

# Eating food

If your endurance is getting low, you can get food to recover 2 **ENDURANCE** points. You cannot do this during a fight and you can only eat one meal per section.

# Your character

This is the first book in the Shadow Thief series. You are Shadow, a young thief of exceptional promise and talent.

If you can survive to the end of this book, your character will be used in future books in the series. Over time, you will learn new skills, grow in ability, and become more adept at your profession.

Therefore, some objects you may find in this adventure, or skills you may choose, may not have relevance in this book, but they may in the future.

Now you are ready to start your adventure.

# Turn to Section 1

The suns are just dropping down over the horizon of the Scarlet Ocean and you know that in a few minutes it will be almost totally dark in the port area in the large, sprawling city of Laeveni. The city is the largest in the empire of the One True God, and contains the holy seat of power. Behind you, as dusk falls, the bells chime from the tall elegant spires of Amaldi City. Amaldi is the central Holy City that resides as an almost separate state inside its own walls in the centre of Laeveni, high on the hillsides. This separate inner city is surrounded by marble walls 50 feet high, and just as thick, and nigh on impregnable. And it is guarded by 5000 warrior monks and priest knights.

The bells chime to call the many priests, monks and acolytes to service in the many hundreds of churches inside the Amaldi walls. The light of the twin suns reflects from the tall marble walls, making the inner city almost seem to gleam. But you are miles away from such grandeur. You will never see inside the walls of the Amaldi City, for to trespass uninvited on church property leads to a very swift, and unpleasant, fate.

However, you ignore the bells and focus. This is your favourite time of the day – when the whole night is in front of you. You carefully suppress the excitement you feel for tonight's job, as excitement leads to haste. You are perched on top of the grain warehouse at the edge of the docks, watching your current prey. You have been watching for the last three nights, knowing that the merchant finishes work at sundown, and then meets fellow merchants in a wine shop for a couple of hours before returning home.

You see merchant Malombr as he leaves his office and warehouse opposite your vantage point on Dockside Way. Malombrs' warehouse looks just like a ramshackle place on Harbour View near the main wharf. He takes time and care to secure his premises. Malombr is a precise man who is never careless. In his time in the town, he has never been robbed despite his wealth being well known. However, he is also a man of routine – which means he is also predictable.

The wharf is getting increasingly lively and rowdy, with sailors in port drinking alongside soldiers, brigands, dwarves and many other creatures in the many dives along the docks. Greasy smoke from the numerous fireplaces and torches lighting the roads drifts up to your vantage point, and mixes with the other smells of a seaport: salt, rotting fish, rubbish, excrement and the stench of unwashed bodies. The docks on a winters evening are not for those with weak stomachs – and that's before you even try the swill the taverns pass off as beer.

He then makes his way away up Harbour View across onto the Street of Blues. He could easily afford to take a coach, but you know he enjoys walking through the filth ridden streets of the wharf. This is partly because he likes to see where he started off as a street urchin, and secondly as he is always on the lookout for a business opportunity and he finds walking gives him the best chance of noting them. He's not worried about run-ins with less desirables, as he's not alone.

As always he's accompanied by his two bodyguards, who are as always half a step behind him, flanking him. These man-mountains look at least half orc.  They are fearsomely muscle and heavily armed with serrated bastard swords sheathed at their hips, along with a number of smaller weapons. You know that a direct confrontation with them would lead to a quick, painful and messy death – for you. Brawn was not an option. As so often in the life of a thief, brains are required.

You follow Malombr and his guards on cat feet, running effortlessly across the rooftops and across streets. You are well-named as you pass like a shadow in the night. Then Malombr turned left onto Willow Street, and follows the road round into Pawnbrokers Avenue. He crosses the square to The One Eyed Rat wine house, leaving his bodyguards outside as the Rat is one of the few places that he doesn't need them. It's also a tavern used by the Thieves Guild.

You wait on the rooftops opposite on the junction with Main Street. You wait in the same position for two hours whilst the merchant eats, drinks and brags with his friends and rivals.

Even the refined area of the more residential areas still carries the stench of the port – although the wine in the Rat is infinitely better than that from the harbour side dives. Then Malombr leaves the Rat, walking quickly and with purpose back home. You get up to follow across the rooftops.

Turn to **73**

Fortunately for you, the guards were not thorough in their search and don't find the Cats Claws hidden in the sleeves of your jerkin. You slip them over your hands, and look up at the 20-foot wall. It is made of roughly laid bricks, with plenty of cracks in the rough mortar between the bricks. As you examine it closely, you shudder as you see broken finger nails and claws embedded in the mortar, obviously left behind by previous less fortunate residents as they tried to escape.

You stare at the wall and plan your route. You listen intently to see if there are guards at the top – but you can hear in the distance laughing and the noise of knuckle bones being thrown on a wooden table. Hopefully the guards are too busy wagering their meagre salary's to bother checking on you. You doubt they would bother to feed you or even give you water, as in a few short hours you will be a dead man walking.

You begin your climb. **TEST YOUR FITNESS**.

Throw 2d6 and if the number is less than or equal to your **FITNESS**, turn to **77**. If it's more than your fitness, turn to **80**

## 3

As you avoid almost certain death entering the tower, your escape has been discovered far earlier than you had hoped. Another group of the City Watch had entered the cell area to find you missing

Within moments, an investigation is underway. Soon on the scene is a tall thin man, who appears to be made up purely of angles. His face is hard, with high slanted cheekbones, a long hook nose and thin lips – which are currently in a half snarl of contempt for the guards – who he quickly orders to be publically flogged at dawn for failing in their duty.

This is a man well known to the Guild, and feared by many - Kaptain Tomas De-Villiers. De-Villiers hates thieves with an almost holy passion, and has made it his life's work to destroy the Guild – and this has led to many of your comrades and friends dancing for the hangman.

He has heard of an upcoming power in the Guild, a young male known only as Shadow, who in 3 years has completed many daring thefts. De-Villiers has been close to catching you before, but this time you were locked up in his cells and have escaped. This has made it personal for De-Villiers. He **WILL** hunt you down this very night and he will not rest until you are strung up by your crooked neck.

He calls for his men – and these are not just the simple strong-arm thugs of the City Watch. These are members of the Black Guard – the Watch's' elite group of trackers and hunters, and rumour has it, sometime assassins. They are a force to be reckoned with.

They arrive mere moments later. De-Villiers gives them their orders, and soon they split up, searching the city for any trace of you. You have precious little time to escape the tower.

Did you have anyone else with you, if so, turn to **23**. If not, turn to **72**

The power of his voice has little effect. Seeing the dark majik in front of you, you decide to take the thief's option. You turn tail and run, as fast as you can up the passageway near the altar. You hear De-Villiers, or whoever it truly is, shriek in rage. You stop and turn and see the ethereal form at the exit of the chamber, but seemingly without his physical body he is trapped in the chamber and unable to follow you. You sprint to the surface.

Turn to **150**

# 5

Wasting no time and leaving the beggar to his own devices, you both flee the guardroom. Behind you, you can hear a series of thuds, as the beggar takes out his anger on the prone guardsmen. The door closes behind you as you leave.

Gain one **FORTUNE** point for successfully escaping – so far.

Turn to **8**

# 6

You hide in the shadows, doing everything you can to stay quiet. The door opens and a pair of burly City Watch walk in. You hope you can try to sneak out of the door, but one stays by the door holding it slightly ajar. You have no chance. You must stay hidden and hope for a better chance to escape later.

**TEST YOUR FORTUNE**. If you are fortunate, turn to **140**. If you are not, turn to **96**

# 7

Finally, the last centipede drops to the floor, its mandibles still chittering together and its segments thrashing from side to side, but eventually it is still. Not wishing to wait to see if there are any more of these behemoths in the nest, you leave quickly. You run to the end of the corridor and then face a choice.

To go straight on, then turn to **67**
Otherwise you must turn left and turn to **103**

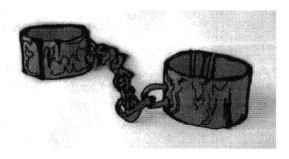

## 8

Jac and you are in a corridor. To the left, several yards away, there is a doorway that is just ajar and you can hear the noise of several men talking and laughing. You think it must be a common room for the off duty City Watch. Knowing that you do not have the strength or ability to take on this many foes, you discount this route. The room is too bright for you to sneak through, even if you have an arcane method of concealment.

To your right is another stout door. Just to the side of this is an alcove. You half drag Jac to the alcove, and tell him that you are going to scout ahead and that he must remain quiet. Before you leave he presses something into your hand. You look down and see it's a ruby pendant. He looks at you and smiles, and closes your fingers around the jewel.

***"Look after this"*** he says ***"and keep it away from HIM. The fate of the city, and the world, depends on this"***

Then he closes his eyes.

You cover him with some rags in the alcove and hope this will suffice.

You try the door, turn to **21**

## 9

Cell 4 is a place of horror. Unlike the other cells you may have seen, this room is packed with instruments of cruelty and torture, and the metallic odour of blood assaults your senses.  In the corner is a Chaos Wheel, a cruel implement that slowly breaks every bone in its victims' bodies. Opposite is a Devils Rack, used to slowly stretch a victim until the sinews of their joints tear.

Cruel hooks are on the walls, each of them dirty with the blood and the morsels of flesh of previous victims. Finally, in the centre you recognise a Dead Man's Coffin, a horizontal iron box with wickedly sharp spikes on the inside walls and lid, and mounted on a pivot. When occupied the coffin can be turned like a spit so that the occupant is constantly falling onto different spikes. Small holes are beneath each spike that allows the blood (and other fluids) to drain away.

The Kaptain of the City Watch has long had a reputation for cruelty and for ends justifying the means. He has been a thorn in the side of the Guild for some time now, and it has always been a source of much speculation how he managed to get such accurate intelligence to combat the Guilds activities. Not many would dare to speak against the Guild for retribution could be swift and deadly.

You stop and consider. Aside from the torturers equipment you can see nothing of interest – except maybe the coffin. The coffin is currently closed. Something is compelling you to open it.

If you decide to open it, turn to **84**

If you decide against it you leave the cell straight away, and you can try
Open Cell 1? Turn to **66**
Open Cell 2? Turn to **53**
Open Cell 3? Turn to **47**
Open Cell 5? Turn to **100**

## 10

You move and roll, but too slowly. You hear a buzzing noise as something flies through the air, and then a sting in your neck. You reach up and pull out a small metal dart. Your blood covers its point, but also you can detect another smell. Then the nerve poison takes hold.

Your promising career as a thief ends here.

# 11

You hear footsteps along the corridor behind you. You stand there frantically trying to open the door, your only route for escape. But the door will not budge. Then you hear shouts behind you and then rough hands grab you and you are clubbed over the head. You awake back in the oubliette, in chains, with guards watching your every move from above.

Turn to **13**

# 12

You lock the grate and using your **SKILL of LOCK PICKING**, jam it so that no one will be able to open it, even with a key. With luck the guards will "sleep" until at least the change of the guard at dawn, and no one will find out about your escape for many hours.

Turn to **60**

There's nothing you can now do. You can see overhead a small barred window in the top of the blockhouse. You watch with creeping horror as the pitch black slowly turns to grey, and then as the dawn breaks through the smog of Laeveni. In your mind's eye you can see the gallows clearly, waiting for you. Your life is now measured in a matter of minutes, not hours.

Shortly the guards open the grate. They put the ladder down and climb into the oubliette. They uncuff you, and you try hopelessly to overpower them but that just earns you a swift smack around the head with a truncheon and you lapse into semi consciousness. You are unceremoniously carried up the ladder by one of the guards, and taken outside and thrown into a barred carriage with several other miscreants.

You are driven up into Hangman's Square and you are taken into a holding cell. From the cell there is a window, overlooking the gallows. Already in the cell are five other occupants. Before leaving one of the guards paints a number 6 on your forehead in red paint. You look round and see the other occupants all have the numbers one to five on their heads, and realise what this means.

After only a few moments, but which seems like a lifetime, the guards come and drag number one away. The poor wretch looks terrified, and pleads with the guards. They laugh in his face, and tell him to save his words for God – as he was going before his judgement. He is dragged off, and you can hear the sounds of the crowds cheering as he is brought to the gibbet. Despite the early hour, a public execution was always a popular attraction in Laeveni.

Over the next minutes, numbers two to five each go to the same fate. Each takes it differently. Two struggles violently and is eventually clubbed unconscious. This gets jeers from the crowd when they don't see a good spectacle as he dies still unconscious. Number three stays silent and impassive, having accepted his fate. Number four prays to his pagan gods and is taken outside looking like he is almost at peace. Number five tries bribery, which just results in more laughs from the guards and a bloody nose.

Then you are by yourself, but not for long, as the guards soon come and take you out into the blinding morning sun. You are half dazzled as you are led up the rough wood steps to the gibbet, where they are just cutting down number fives still twitching corpse. You are quickly taken and the noose placed over your head. You are not offered a blindfold (the crowd love to see the faces of the condemned as they die), and not allowed anytime to speak.

The Magistrate says a few short words, saying you had been found guilty of attempted larceny. You have been tried in your absence in accordance with the norms of Laeveni. Then the crowd goes silent in anticipation.

The Executioner reaches for the level to open the trap. You can only hope the fall is clean and breaks your neck to kill you instantly. But again fate is playing with you. Due to your sleight frame, the drop is not enough and instead you suffer the pain and indignity of one final dance. Ironically, the last face you see in this life is Malombr, as he has stopped on his way to work to watch the show, shadowed as ever by his guards.

When you finally stop kicking, you are cut down and thrown on a cart with the others. The cart then takes your bodies to a pit outside the city walls, and you are thrown in a mass grave and buried without a marker.

Your promising career as a thief ends here.

You effortlessly unlock the large but very rudimentary lock. It clicks as it opens, and the noise seems to echo through the room above you. You hear the sounds of chairs scraping, as they are pushed back, and then the heavy tread of booted feet. You see two guards emerge from a lit room. They walk past the oubliette grate, and you hold your breath in case they look down to see you hanging there like a spider. They don't, and walk out of your line of vision. Then you hear a noise, a sort of signal, and the sound of a door opening. A bright shaft of light arrows into the room, and mirrored on the wall near you, you see the shadows of the two guards walk through the door. Then it closes and the light is gone. The room seems empty. Now is your chance.

You brace your body you manage to heave the heavy grate up a foot to allow you to scramble under. You notice some hay and dark sacking in the corner, and quickly stuff some hay in a couple of sacks, tied with a rope and throw it down the oubliette.

With luck, if the guards return and check they will mistake the hay in dark sacks as your prone body and even if they try to unlock the grate to investigate they will struggle. Hopefully they will not know you have gone until dawn – and this will only add to your legend when news gets out that a suspected thief simply disappeared from a locked cell without a trace.

Turn to **60**

# 15

Your trick works and both the guards fall forward and onto the floor, their hands out in front of them to try to catch them. They both land on caltrops, and the venom of the scarlet water snake causes instant paralysis of both of the guards. You run to the door as it starts to close, and manage to keep it open. Wasting no time and leaving the beggar to his own devices, you both flee the guardroom. Behind you, you can hear a series of thuds, as the beggar takes out his anger on the prone guardsmen.

Turn to **8**

# 16

**TEST YOUR INTELLIGENCE** but you can take 2 away from the roll due to your **LOCK PICK** abilities.

If you roll less than or equal, turn to **89**
If you fail, turn to **22**

# 17

You remember as you hide in the corner that you found a dark cloak in the cells and this may help you hide. You quickly find it in your bag, and shroud yourself in it. Then you use all your training to become almost preternaturally still. You try to slow your breathing and are almost in a trance like state.

You can still hear the footsteps and the murmuring voices from the other side of the door, which then opens. Two members of the city watch come through. One of the guards stands holding the door open, whilst the other walks across the room. You hope neither see you.

Fortunately, you have found a Cloak of Night, a charmed garment that works to throw light away from the wearer, and make them imperceptible to the naked eye. Legend has it these Cloaks can hide a man in daylight, unless the sun shines directly on the wearer, or if they are in a brightly lit room.

It seems to work as the guard goes into another room and emerges with some sheaves of paper. Then they both leave the way they came, and the door locks behind them.

You decide you will have to see what's beyond the iron gate.

Turn to **91**

# 18

You see no option but try to sneak out via the main door, or wait until the master returns to his home. You decide to try your fortune with the door. Turn to **132**

# 19

*"Ah, we have a rabbit. A quick rabbit, but I am quicker. I am a hawk"* shouts Celdron as he darts his blade towards you. The thin point pierces your side and you drop to the floor in agony. Then Celdron is on you, and he binds you so you cannot move.

*"Well done Celdron, you were quick, and I wanted him taken alive, to question below. Take him below to Cell 4. I will question him in detail. Heat up the coals and sharpen my tools. It is going to be a long night"*

A quick death would have been fortunate, but you are now going to endure a night of pain and torment. Your promising career as a thief ends here

# 20

You leave, locking the cell door as you exit. If you haven't already, will you?

Open Cell 1? Turn to **66**
Open Cell 2? Turn to **53**
Open Cell 3? Turn to **47**
Open Cell 4? Turn to **49**
Open Cell 5? Turn to **100**

The door is locked! Do you have a set of iron keys, if you do, turn to **89**.

If you do not, if you have the ability of **PICK LOCK**, turn to **16**.

If you have neither, turn to **22**

## *22*

**TEST YOUR FORTUNE,** but add 1 to the roll. If you succeed, turn to **89**.

If you fail, turn to **11**

## *23*

You hear the commotion below and realise the alarm has been raised. You can do nothing more for Jac, you will just have to hope he uses his skill to remain hidden whilst the guards search for you. You offer a prayer to the pagan God of Thieves, hoping that you and Jac will meet again. If for no other reason than the money, he now owes you.

Turn to **72**

## 24

You kick the rat out of the way and it scurries out of the cell. You uncover your arm, and see the twin fang marks in your bicep – like small vampire bites. You calm your mind and place your other hand over the bite and concentrate.

You can feel the disease already entering your bloodstream, but you can focus your body's natural defences against this area. As you concentrate you feel the area warm, until it becomes almost too hot to touch. You have successfully destroyed the disease inside you, but at a cost.

Lose **1 ENDURANCE** point as this treatment has sapped your body.

Will you now:

Open Cell 1? Turn to **66**
Open Cell 2? Turn to **53**
Open Cell 4? Turn to **49**
Open Cell 5? Turn to **100**

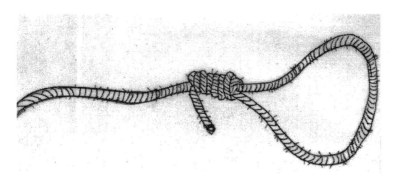

## 25

Sadly, his period of confinement and lack of nutrition have left Jac unable to defeat his foe. You stop briefly and say a quick prayer to the ancient God of Thieves. Before you go you quickly search his body and find a ruby pendant hidden in an inside pocket. You also find a set of keys on one of the guards. You leave through the door as quick as you can – before anyone else arrives.
Turn to **55**

# 26

The Guard Room is a small, scruffy room, with a table and chairs, a fire and couple of upright bureaus with papers strewn all over them and some cluttered shelves. On the table are the remnants of the guard's supper and knucklebone games. There is enough food for 2 meals if you want to take it. You can also take the knucklebones and the 3 gold pieces' worth of small coin from the table.

On a hook by the door is a set of iron keys – probably for the various cells.

Do you want to:
Search the bureau and shelves for anything useful. Turn to **61**
Take the set of keys. Turn to **85**
Leave and creep up to the large door and try to open it.  Turn to **71**
Leave and head down the corridor. Turn to **74**

# 27

As you leap, your stiff calf muscles betray you. You lack the strength in your legs to take off and your arms cartwheel as you try futilely to propel yourself through the air toward the opposite roof. You brush the edge of the gutter with your fingertips, but this is not enough. You cannot stop yourself from falling and you end up crashing to the cobbled streets, 15 feet below. If you have the **SKILL of AGILITY**, you manage to break your fall and only suffer **2 ENDURANCE** damage. If you don't have the **SKILL of AGILITY**, deduct 4 points from your **ENDURANCE**.

The fates are definitely playing games with you as you quickly turn over to find yourself looking up at a detachment of the City Watch, all of whom are pointing their rusty but still lethal swords at your throat. They haul you to your feet, and roughly search you and quickly realise your profession. Without time to protest you are put into manacles and marched off to the nearest blockhouse – which is ominously on Execution Hill, on the somewhat inappropriately named Dead Man's Row.

Unless you can find a way to escape, come morning you will be dancing on the end of a rope. Justice in recent times has become swift in Laeveni, and demands little proof.

Turn to **34**

## 28

You are faced with a dead end but on the floor is an old backpack, possibly dropped by a looter or adventurer from ages ago. You rummage through the pack and find a small bottle. Its contents glow red, the colour normally denotes a potion of **FIGHTING SKILL**. You put this in your backpack. If you drink it, it will add 1 to your **FIGHTING SKILL** for one fight only – even to exceed 12. Now you must double back and take the other tunnel.
Turn to **135**

## 29

*"Welcome, young thief"* says De Villiers in a voice that is rich and commanding *"you have been a difficult man to find. But now you have come to me, yes? I can feel that you have something for me. Would you like to hand it over?*

*Of course you will be richly rewarded - for he who delivers the last key to free My Master from his unjust imprisonment will be lauded above all else. You will live a long life and be rich beyond your dreams. Come, hand it over".*

Your will is crumbling. You feel your hand reaching into your backpack.

Do you have a **RUBY AMULET**, if so then turn to **120**
If you have a **SIGIL OF DEATH**, then turn to **106**
If you have neither of these, turn to **46**

**30**

The guards stop uncertainly. They are more used to dealing with drunks and whores down the seafront, not being asked to investigate a crime by such a powerful member of society. Even more so, they are worried when you mention the name of De-Villiers – as he is not a kindly boss.

*"Calm down, good sir"* says the foremost guard, who by the grey streaks in his hair seems to be the most senior of the Watch

*"My condolences, sir. Can you give me your name again sir, and some brief details, but there's nothing that can be done about it tonight. We are short staffed enough as it is, with those dwarves traveling to their annual moot in the hills and stopping over in Laeveni, just as a group of goblins arrive in town. You can imagine the fighting in the taverns. We're hard pressed sir"*

Realising you don't have the time for a prolonged conversation you need to get out quickly, as at any moment they may notice the oubliette.

So thinking fast, you say *"If you are too busy to help, then I will find the Kaptain myself. Out of my way!"*

You barge past the Watchman nearest you who looks flabbergasted and you head towards the one holding the door open, intend you flounce past him and out of the door. But he steps forward towards you, hands up, trying to placate you. You see the door start to swing shut. You only have moments. You dash towards the door, but too late as the door swings into the frame, and there a click as it locks.

You turn around and smile at the guards rather sheepishly. Their faces become hard as it dawns on them that you were trying to trick them and that you are the thief.

You must fight them both, but for the first two rounds, you must increase each guards **FIGHTING SKILL** by 1, as they are so enraged by your attempted deception. You must also lose 1 **FIGHTING SKILL**, as you only have one dagger to fight with.

GUARD 1      **FIGHTING SKILL 8**   **ENDURANCE 9**
GUARD 1      **FIGHTING SKILL 7**   **ENDURANCE 8**

If your endurance gets down to 2 or less, turn to **44**.

If you kill them both, you find the door locked and decide to try the iron gate.

Turn to **91**

## 31

You grab Jac and half drag him through the door. He is hardly able to stand and you realise he is exhausted. If you take him with you, then you will lose all hope of escaping. You resolve you must find a place to keep him safe, in the hope that you can sneak out and find a way to help him later.

Turn to **8**

## 32

Too slow, the door opens and you are still only halfway across the room. The first watchman, who is standing keeping the door open, sees you and shouts **"Oi, you, stop"**. You have nowhere to go, and are outnumbered 2 to 1.

Do you have the **SKILL** of **CHARM AND GUILE**
If so, turn to **52**
If you don't, turn to **44**

## 33

You crouch down to the floor and examine the man's remains. He was obviously a mighty warrior, as he must be at least 6 and a half feet tall, with a massive ribcage that pokes through the rusted mail coat. His amour is far too large and useless. You look closely and see that there are what seems to be gnawing marks, made by sharp teeth, or something else, on the visible bones. This man hasn't just rotted over a long time, he was eaten. You fight down a wave of disgust.

Next to him is a backpack. You look inside and all that is salvageable is a small green glass bottle. You decide to take it - it's a potion of **FORTUNE** that will increase your current **FORTUNE** by one (even surpassing your initial value) for one roll only.

You stow it away in your bag and return to the junction. As you turn to leave, your foot strikes against something solid just under the surface. You bend down and poke around and your hand closes on the hilt of a sword. You pull it free, and strike the blade against the stone wall. It rings true, and the dirt and muck falls from it to reveal a shining longsword. Despite its size it is beautifully balanced even for one of your slender build and seems to have little weight. You have found a sword made of Antium, the lightest and strongest steel ever produced. Even master smiths and the dwarves have lost the knowledge to produce this steel. It is a fine weapon indeed, and worth a small fortune.

When using the Antium Sword you can add +2 to your **FIGHTING SKILL.** To go straight on, turn to **145**, or to turn left, turn to **111**

## 34

You are marched to the gaol on near Hangman's Square and stripped of all your effects and thrown into an oubliette wearing only your hose, jerkin and boots. The guards throw down the heavy metal grate and secure it with a large lock. You are now in the dark, 20 feet below the grate, in a floor covered in straw and human waste, sharing your new accommodation only with a number of scurrying rats.

If you have the **CLIMB** skill, turn to **77**. If you do not turn to **2**

## 35

The ground seems to be softer in this passageway as you slowly move down it, as it's getting ever darker. Then all of a sudden your feet slide from underneath you as they slip on the ground - but then you realise it's not you slipping, it's the ground moving. A sink hole has opened up and is dragging the soft sandy earth into it.

You scramble to try to escape the pull of this dreadful hole, but your hands cannot get any purchase on any solid ground and you slip and slide inexorably towards your doom. It feels like minutes you fight the tide of the earth, but it's only a few seconds and then you are pulled into the sink hole and fall, to be buried in a tomb of earth forever. Your promising career as a thief ends here

## 36

Malombr crosses the Market Square and moves down Market Street and then turns right into Anvil Street. You wait at the junction, as his house is just over the road and you don't want to alert him – now that the streets are quieter. You listen and hear as he unlocks the door and it creaks open. A few moments later it shuts, and you can hear a number of locks being engaged. You know from watching that the front door is tough to crack – as it is now locked internally when the master is in residence. But you have another route planned.

You slip around the corner and almost collide with one of Malombrs hulking bodyguards. They must have spotted you following and Malombr must have left him behind to catch you. You have walked right into their trap!

He towers above you, a good 18 inches taller than you, and has his evil serrated sword ready in his hand. It gleams wickedly in the moonlight. You have no time to react, as he slowly and with great pleasure runs you through. His aim is not for the heart for a quick death but for the stomach to make it last.

The blade is so sharp there is hardly any pain when it slides in. However, then the man-beast slices downwards into your intestines and pulls the blade out unhurriedly. The serrated edges catch on your entrails and pull them out of the now gaping hole in your torso. The pain is immense and you scream out once, and then go into shock and fall to your knees in a puddle of your own blood and innards. Then the huge creature quickly places a rough noose of hemp rope around your desk and drags you do the nearest lamp stand.

He flings the end of the rope over the crossbeam and pulls. You scream once more as you are hoisted off the ground and left dangling six foot above the ground with your innards trailing down to the floor. He ties off the rope, and then dips his fingers into your guts, and writes on the wall in your own blood "**THIEF"**. You gurgle as the rope cuts into your neck and crushes your larynx. You pant, trying to get your breathe, but it is no good and eventually your face turns first red then purple.

You eventually lose consciousness as the life slips from you. Your corpse remains strung up on the post for some weeks – and becomes a welcome meal for the scavengers that live in the city. Soon there is little left of you but yellowing bone, but you remain strung up there as a warning not to try to steal from Malombr. Your adventure ends, rather messily, here. As does your promising career as a thief.

## 37

If you have a set of iron keys, you can try to open the gate, then turn to **91**

If not, you will have to trust to luck and try to pick the lock. **TEST YOUR FORTUNE**. If you are successful, turn to **91**. If you are not, turn to **64**

## 38

Neither of you are strong enough to successfully get either of the guards to fall onto the caltrops. They turn with surprising speed for their bulk, and raise their cudgels. However, one of the caltrops rolls over the floor to the door, which is starting to close. It gets lodged under the bottom edge of the door, and keeps it wedged open. You have a chance to escape, but first you must defeat the guards.

You must fight guard 1, whilst Jac must fight guard 2. You throw Jac one of your stilettos as hand to hand in his weakened state he wouldn't stand a chance. You must reduce your **FIGHTING SKILL** by 1 for fighting only with one knife.

You must fight both as Jac and yourself, each engaging a guard. Roll 1d6. If it's odd, you fight guard 1. If it's even, you fight guard 2. If one of you kills your guard first, then you can both attack the remaining guard the next round. If Jac's dies before killing his guard, then you must fight them both.

| | | |
|---|---|---|
| **JAC** | **FIGHTING SKILL 9** | **ENDURANCE 6** |
| **GUARD 1** | **FIGHTING SKILL 8** | **ENDURANCE 9** |
| **GUARD 2** | **FIGHTING SKILL 7** | **ENDURANCE 8** |

If you manage to defeat both guards, turn to **87**

## 39

Years of thievery recognises that noise, the sound of a trip wire. Without thinking you move in the way you think would be most unpredictable, you throw yourself backwards.

This saves you as a giant spiked ball on the chain whistles past your nose from one side to the other. If you had remained where you were it would likely have taken your head off or broken your back. You stop and wait whilst the ball slowly loses momentum and comes to a halt, directly in front of you. You duck under, hook it out of the way over a nearby lamp holder, and close the door and continue into the tower.

Turn to **3**

## 41

You are back in the corridor outside the cells but you have spent too long searching. You hear the front door start to open. You swear under your breath. Are you alone?

If you are, turn to **64**. If you are not, turn to **62**

## 42

There is no obvious exit from this tower apart from the door you came in. You head back to the door and listen but you can still hear activity outside. There must be another way out!

You search around. If you have the **SKILL of SIXTH SENSE**, turn to **83**
If you do not, **TEST YOUR FORTUNE**. If you are fortunate, turn to **83**. If you are not, turn to **18**

## 43

Malombr moves cautiously through the street. No one has the nerve to get in the way of his hideous guards but he is clearly being a lot more careful than on previous nights – probably due to your little mishap on the roof. You follow him along the rooftops, as quiet as your namesake, a shadow. As you cross into the merchant district, you drop back to the ground and follow at street level. You don't need to follow too closely as you know exactly where he is heading – his townhouse.

Turn to **36**

# 44

You are caught by the guards. They struggle to open the oubliette but manage, and cuff you, before throwing you back down. You land in a heap on the floor, even your thieves reflexes are unable you to effect a safe landing. Lose 2 **ENDURANCE**. This time, guards remain at the top of the oubliette, watching you. There is no escape.

Turn to **13**

# 45

You turn back, your heart racing with fear. In the coffin, the body is moving. The head is rolling from side to side, the good eye is flickering open and closed, and the red gash that is now what the mouth was is opening and closing. Faint words can be heard coming from these torn lips.

Instead of fear, you feel overwhelming pity for this poor girl, as she must have suffered more than practically anyone you have ever met. You take out your skin of small beer, and pour some onto her parched lips. The liquid burns her lips but she is still thankful for the liquid and you give her more.

You move closer to her mouth, bending over the coffin. She half whispers, half croaks, and her eye flickers in recognition.

*"You.....I ......know.......You are..........the one called. .....*
*Shadow".*

You nod your head.

*"I am In....ista"* she continues. You nod again – she is a lesser magic user who has recently opened a shop in the Alley of Rumours – close to one of the Guilds headquarters. She has become well known in the Guild for providing potions and charms, as well as information on her clients that were suitable targets for the Guild. The Kaptain must have taken her and tortured her. She had not been seen for three days.

*"Yes I know you – I can help"* you say. She shakes her head and cuts you off.

*"It's….too late for……….. that now…..my mortal…body is doomed……but my spirit will…………live on. Before you go……know this……"*

Then she coughs and splutters, blood foaming from her mouth. Then she seems to rally and find a final desperate strength.

*"There….is a great,,,,,evil in Laeveni. The man in charge of this blockhouse is one of …. Its chief lieutenants… but the true head of the dragon has yet to be revealed. You must stop this power, as it threatens not just the Guild, but the whole of Laeveni itself….even Most Holy……Visit the Apothecary on Singing Avenue, and ask for Livia. She can tell you more"*

And then she is gone. If you want to say a quick prayer to the heathen God of Thieves and close her eyes before you go then turn to **129**

If you decide you need to make haste and leave this room, turn to **41**

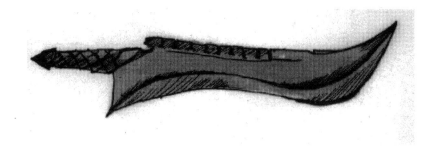

## 46

You reach into your backpack and then remove your fist. You extend it towards De-Villiers and open it, palm up, to reveal …

Nothing

*"You have it not? You fool! I have passed eons waiting for this moment and will not be defeated. It is time for Him to rise again. Where is it? I will cut its location from you flesh"*

Then from inside his robe he draws a sabre like blade and a short, hooked knife made of volcanic glass. The knife is old with age but still looks razor sharp.

**DE-VILLIERS**　　　**FIGHTING SKILL 11**　　　**ENDURANCE 13**

Each time De-Villiers hits you, throw 1d6. If it's even, then his sword hurts you and does the usual 2 **ENDURANCE** damage, but if it's odd, the knife hurts you. The knife is the sacrificial blade that has been used for centuries and has an evil, but fickle, power, which makes it unpredictable. With each attack from the knife, roll 1d6 and this the damage it does to your **ENDURANCE**.

If you win, turn to **114**. If you lose, turn to **108**

## 47

Cell 3 is empty, or at least you think it is. As you cross the doorway, an extra-large rat jumps down from the ceiling beam and bites you on the arm. Its extra-long teeth are able to piece your jerkin sleeves. Lose 2 points of **ENDURANCE**. You curse. Like many things in Laeveni, even the rats are dangerous, as they often carry the Dropping Sickness. This disease can come on in moments or hours later, and can cause a loss of balance and coordination, sickness, weakness and even death.

Do you have the **SKILL of CHAKRA**? If so turn to **24**. If not, lose **2 ENDURANCE** and **1 FITNESS** points now and you may need to find an apothecary as soon as possible. You leave the cell cursing under your breath.

Will you now:

Open Cell 1? Turn to **66**
Open Cell 2? Turn to **53**
Open Cell 4? Turn to **49**
Open Cell 5? Turn to **100**

# 48

**TEST YOUR FORTUNE**, but your **SKILL of AGILITY** allows you to only add 3 to your roll.

If you are successful, turn to **63**. If you are not so fortunate, turn to **27**

# 49

You open and enter Cell 4 and immediately your senses are assailed by the stench of what can only be described as suffering.

If you decide to leave, turn back to **20** if you want to search another cell

If you decide against your better judgement to enter, turn to **9**

# 50

You slowly creep up the stairs, staying to the side in case there is a loose floorboard given to creaking in the centre. You get to the landing, and there are three more doors off it. You quickly check them but find nothing of interest in any of them. You have wasted your time.

Lose **1 FORTUNE** point.

You walk down the stairs back to the hallway. If you haven't already, you can try the left hand door, then turn to **65**, or the right hand door, turn to **98**

## 51

The lock is a simple one and soon gives way to your skill.

Turn to **91**

## 52

You stop and smile at the guards, and bow graciously. Then, effecting the best courtier's manners you can, you speak to the guards. ***"Thank The One True God, I was desperately looking for you gentlemen. My names is Malombr and I am a Merchant of some repute. You may have heard of me. I am in trouble; I have been robbed! Some cad has broken into my house and stolen all my gold! Is the Kaptain De-Villiers here? As I need to report it as soon as possible and I know the good Kaptain as he is a regular at my parties"***

**TEST your FORTUNE**. Take 2 away from the result. If the result is less than or equal to your current **FORTUNE**, then you have convinced them – and turn to **30**.

If the result is greater than your current **FORTUNE**, the Watch are not fooled by your deception and realise you are a thief attempting to escape. You have no choice but to fight them both.

Turn to **76**

You approach the second cell, and peer through the dark. A shape is slumped against the caged back wall, not moving. You carefully unlock the cell, keeping your eyes on the shape all the time, and then open the door and enter. Sitting in the corner is a man just a few years older than you – and as he raises his matted head, you get a jolt of recognition as you recognise the filthy face looking up at you – despite the blood and bruises that are evidence of a good beating.

You whisper *"Lightning Jac – is that you?"* The man smiles back exhaustedly and nods. Jac is a member of the Guild who disappeared on an important job for the Guild Master a few nights ago. And now here he is, half naked and half-starved in a cell. You throw him one of your provisions (remember to deduct that from your adventure sheet) which Jac catches with astonishing reflexes – despite his current condition. He wolfs down the food, whilst you unlock his chains.

He gets up and stumbles with weakness, but soon the food starts to take effect and he's more stable. Then he goes to the back of the cell and starts to dig around.

*"There's no time to talk now Jac, I have just escaped from this place myself and the guards could come back at any time. Let's get out of here".*

*"Wait, wait, it must be here, it must. I hid it here and would not tell them"* he mutters, and then in triumph he finds what he had hidden. You see a glitter of gold and the gleam of a red jewel as he places it inside his tunic.

*"You wasted time for a bit of loot? Are you soft in the head? You can always steal more. Time to go"* you whisper urgently.

Jac nods and you make your way to the staircase.

For rescuing Jac, he is now in your debt. For the next 169 days, as Guild tradition dictates, he must split half of his haul with you in thanks for his liberation. As Jac is one of the best thief's in the Guild, this should earn you a tidy sum.

Add one **FORTUNE** point to your current **FORTUNE** score.
You Jac in his cell with some more food and small beer to recover
whilst you search the other cells.

If you haven't already, you can:

Open Cell 1? Turn to **66**
Open Cell 3? Turn to **47**
Open Cell 4? Turn to **49**
Open Cell 5? Turn to **100**

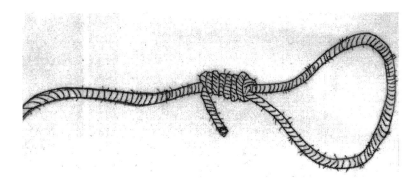

## 54

Your eyes happen upon an old black cloak that's draped over an
empty barrel. It looks moth eaten and soiled, but you can sense
something about it. You pick it up, and examine it closely. It is of
unusually fine weave, and almost seems to manage to be darker
than its surrounding, so that it's quite difficult to see.

Your eyes almost seem to slip off it and focus upon something else.
There's definitely something arcane about it. If you decide to take it
to examine later, stow the black cloak into your bag
If not if you haven't already done so you can check the other cells.

Open Cell 1? Turn to **66**
Open Cell 2? Turn to **53**
Open Cell 3? Turn to **47**
Open Cell 4? Turn to **49**

# 55

You are in a corridor. To the left, several yards away, there is a doorway that is just ajar and you can hear the noise of several men talking and laughing.

You think it must be a common room for the off duty City Watch. Knowing that you do not have the strength or ability to take on this many foes. The room looks brightly lit and you have no chance of sneaking through, even with arcane means. You discount this route.

To your right is another stout door. You try the door, turn to **21**

# 56

**TEST YOUR INTELLIGENCE**. If you have the **SKILL of LOCK PICKING** you can subtract 1 from your roll. If you succeed turn to **88**. Otherwise you fail and get bored of searching the room and leave.

If you try the right hand other door, turn to **98**, or if you would prefer to go upstairs, turn to **50**.

If you have had enough of this place and want to try to find a way out, turn to **42**

# 57

You react a fraction of a second too late, and are smashed in the chest by a huge spiked iron ball which swings down on a chain from the ceiling. It has been released by the trip wire you unfortunately triggered. It thuds into you with tremendous impact, shattering your ribs as you half turn to meet it. You are thrown sideways against the wall, hitting it with more bone splintering force and drop to the ground unmoving.

Your promising career as a thief ends here

## 58

You are back in the hallway. If you haven't already, do you want to try the right hand door, then turn to **98**, or if you would prefer to go upstairs, turn to **50**.

If you want to try to leave the tower turn to **42**

## 59

You quickly rummage through the contents of the make-do storeroom.
Do you have the **SKILL of DIVVY**? If so turn to **54**

If not, you find nothing of interest and you decide to leave the cell.
If not if you haven't already done so you can check the other cells.

Open Cell 1? Turn to **66**
Open Cell 2? Turn to **53**
Open Cell 3? Turn to **47**
Open Cell 4? Turn to **49**

## 60

The rest of this level of the blockhouse seems empty and so you have a bit of time. You look around the room, and find your effects have just been thrown onto a table nearby. You grab them and hastily stow them away around your personage. You hear the night watch ring the time. Only an hour has passed since your capture! Your plan could still work! Add 1 **FORTUNE** point.

You look at the layout of the blockhouse. Ahead of you up some steps is a heavy door that looks like the exit from this room. About 10 foot above and to the left of this door is a window, and you can see the night sky.

Your heart leaps as you never thought you would see that sight again. You quickly push down all emotion. Now is a time for clear thinking and logic.

To the right there is the guard room and you can see through the open door a table containing food, drink and knucklebones. There are even a few coins on the table – from the guards gambling. To the left is a corridor, but this is barred by an iron gate.

What do you want to do now? Do you?
Enter the guard room and search it? Turn to **26**
Creep up to the large door and try to open it? Turn to **71**
Head down the corridor? Turn to **74**

You quickly look through the piles of parchment strewn about on the bureaus and shelves. The guards are clearly not the best at paperwork. However, one of the bureaus has a locked drawer – which is child's play for you to open. You slowly pull the drawer open, in case there is a trap, and can see a sheaf of papers.

They are a combination of arrest warrants and free passage warrants, already stamped in wax and affixed with the crest of Kaptain De-Villiers. There are names on the warrants, but you know a clever little trick to remove ink so that names can be rewritten. These could be invaluable. You store them in your backpack – make sure you note them on your Adventure Sheet.

If you haven't already done so, you can now either:
Take the set of keys? Turn to **85**
Leave the room and try the large wooden door, turn to **71**
Leave the room and head down the corridor, turn to **74**

## *62*

Both yours and Jacs lightening reflexes save you and you are able to move quickly and quietly to either side of the door before it opens. Jac and you communicate quickly in Thief's-talk, a silent method of communication known to all Guild member that uses only small hand movements to convey a lot of information quickly. You both know your roles. You reach into your bag and find a set of caltrops and cast them quickly on the floor.

A pair of burly City Watch come into the room, half carrying, half dragging a semi-conscious beggar. As soon as they are past the door, you both step behind them and using an old wrestling trick, you trip them up and push them forwards. **TEST YOUR FORTUNE**. You use your current **FORTUNE**, Jac has a current **FORTUNE** score of 7 (he's had a bad week).

If you both are fortunate, turn to **15**
If only one of you is fortunate, turn to **68**
If you are both unlucky, turn to **38**

# 63

You leap and are just able to catch the edge of the next building, but your landing is far from silent. Your foot catches a roof tile, which falls to the ground and smashes against the cobbled streets. You managed to roll onto the rooftop quickly, as Malombr is stopped by his guards, who both reach for their swords as they look for the source of the unexpected sound. Tense moments that seem like minutes pass by, until the guards are certain there is no threat to their master. However, you swear silently – knowing that your quarry has now been alerted. This could make things more complicated.

Turn to **43**

# 64

You hear a key grate into the lock of the large wooden door. Your lightening reflexes save you and you are able to move quickly and quietly into a corner before you hear movement on the other side of the large door, and keys in a lock. The door inches open and torchlight flickers through the gap, and you hide back in the shadows, covering your face.

Do you have the **SKILL of HIDING IN SHADOW**? If so turn to **6**
If you have a ragged old black cloak, turn to **17**

If you don't, **TEST YOUR FORTUNE**. If you are lucky, turn to **6**. If you are not, turn to **32**

# 65

You move quietly to the left hand door and place your ear against it. Again all is silent. Suspicious after the trip wire, you check the door frame for any signs of traps but cannot see anything. You place your hand on the door handle and slowly turn.

Turn to **78**

You walk up to the first cell. The cell is all in shadow and even your excellent night vision cannot determine if the cell is empty or occupied. The corridor is eerily quiet, and the main things you can hear are the rats scurrying around your feet and the occasional crackling of the smoky torches. You try the first key, and it unlocks the cell with a dull clunk. You open the door, and the rusted hinges protest noisily. You creep into the cell and your vision adjusts and you can see a shadow against the wall – a male figure hangs from his arms from the back wall. His feet and arms are manacled to the walls. You watch for a few moments to determine if he is still alive, and then can see his naked scarred and skinny chest moving in and out almost imperceptivity.

You walk over and lift his head by the matted filthy hair. Almost imperceptivity, he groans "*help me"* through dry, cracked lips as you look into his face – a face that is more straggly beard than anything else. His eyes flicker open, deep set in his almost cadaverous face – a face with paper thin skin drawn tight over bones due to sustained malnourishment.

Have you got the **SKILL** of **SIXTH SENSE**? If you do turn to **70**
If not, do you:
Try to use one of the keys to and free the wretch? Turn to **90**
Leave the cell, and the poor wretch to his suffering? Turn to **97**

Another junction. Will this labyrinth never cease? If you escape this journey you vow never to go underground again. Your choices are turn left or go right. You peer down the left passage. It curves out of sight after a few yards and so you cannot tell how long it goes on for, but the air seems dead and stale. To the right, the passage is high, with vaulted ceilings made out of old, dark, bricks. On the sides of the walls there are deposits of a grey semi-liquid, semi-solids, that streak down the walls. You poke at it with your finger, and smell it. It's got a musty, peppery smell to it. It reminds you of the powder used in war canons. Clearly some creature lives down this tunnel. If you want to take a sample, add it to your adventure sheet as guano.

Having examined your options, you can now either go left and turn to **28**, or head right and turn to **135**

## 68

One of the guards falls and lands on the venomous caltrops and is paralysed almost instantly. The other just stumbles but stays upright. You must fight him. Jac is unarmed and relatively useless in this fight as he is so weak, but he is able to grab the door and stop it from closing tight.

**GUARD 1      FIGHTING SKILL 8   ENDURANCE 9**

If you win two combat rounds in a row, turn to **95**
If you win any other way, turn to **5**

## 69

You flee the cell as fast as your legs will carry you. Startled by what you have seen; you decide to leave this unholy blockhouse straight away. But you cannot find a way past the locked door. You must have missed something in one of the cells. You go back to check.

Open Cell 1? Turn to **66**
Open Cell 2? Turn to **53**
Open Cell 3? Turn to **47**
Open Cell 4? Turn to **49**

## 70

Years of putting your life and freedom on the line each and every night have given you this sense – that something is wrong. You step back, and look more closely at the cell and its occupant. The manacles shine with a silvery light, even in this dark environment – and you reach up and touch them. You gasp! They are silver – a metal far too valuable to be used to hang a common thief or beggar. Your education has included elements of the supernatural and you remember that silver has power over some of the (many) types of undead creatures – including vampires, were-creatures, wight's and ghouls.

You hastily leave the cell, locking the door. Back in the cell, the Wight raises its head and stares at your departing figure with a terrible hunger burning in its eyes. You have narrowly escaped a nasty and painful death.

Turn to **97**

## 71

The door is large, made of oak and bound with steel. You try your best to open it, but it is too solid. There is also no locking mechanism on this side, no key hole, and no way to pick the lock. You realise that the door must have to be opened from the outside only, maybe by a pre-arranged signal. You decide it's not worthwhile trying to find the signal, as there are bound to be guards on the other side, even if the door is opened for you.

You can now either:
If you haven't already, search the guard room, turn to **26**
Head down the corridor to the metal gate, turn to **74**

## 72

Despite knowing you are being chased, you realise that haste will lead to an almost certain death – the tower has already proven to be protected via traps. You stop and check your surroundings. The hallway is quite simple, with a straight wooden staircase at the end and a door off to the left and the right. You listen. Nothing. That makes sense as the tripwire is unlikely to be activated if the owner of the tower was in residence. Will you:

Go up the stairs, turn to **50**
Open the door to the left, turn to **65**; or
Open the door to the right, turn to **98**

## 73

You have neglected to keep your body subtle and ready for action whilst waiting. You curse yourself as you get up and find your calf muscles are tense and stiff. You almost stumble as you set off across the rooftop and then have to jump across an alley onto the other side of the street.

If you have the **SKILL of AGILITY**, turn to **48**. If you do not, **TEST YOUR FORTUNE** but add 4 to the role. If you are lucky, turn to **63**. If you are unlucky, turn to **27**

## 74

You reach the iron gate which blocks the way and try to open it. It's locked.

If you have the **SKILL of LOCK PICKING**, turn to **51**. If you do not, turn to **37**

## 75

The descent continues, and once more you are faced with a decision. There is a passageway to the left, or you can carry on straight. The left passage has a kind of musty smell to it, whereas the route straight on descends even steeper into darkness.

If you decide to turn left, turn to **135**. If you carry straight on, turn to **139**

## 76

Both guards circle on you. The one near the door moves forward and the door swings shut with a click as the locking mechanism sets. You are armed with both your stilettos against 2 guards armed with cudgels. You must fight them both together, and can only injure one guard per attack round, even if your **FIGHTING SKILL** is higher.

**GUARD 1**   **FIGHTING SKILL 8**   **ENDURANCE 9**
**GUARD 1**   **FIGHTING SKILL 7**   **ENDURANCE 8**

If your endurance gets down to 2 or less, turn to **44**. If you kill them both, you search them quickly but find only a set of iron keys. If you have no keys you can keep them. You try the door, but its locked firm. You decide to try to open the iron gate. Turn to **91**

## 77

You climb the rough walls like a spider, soon getting to the top and grabbing hold of the grate. The gaps between the bars are more than big enough for you to get your arm through. You hook your arm around the bars and hang from it, bracing yourself with your feet against the sides of the wall. Fortunately, the walls have narrowed and so you can put one foot each side and hold a lot of weight on your feet. You know that you can easily hold this position for at least 6 minutes, but you still have to hurry. You manage to bring your left leg towards you so that you can get your lock pick tools from the false stitching in your boot heel.

If you have the **SKILL** of **LOCK PICKING** turn to **14**. If you do not, turn to **86**

## 78

The door swings open effortlessly as you turn the handle. The room is clearly a study. A large leather topped desk dominates the room, with an ornate high back chair behind it. The curtains are drawn and the room is dark, lit only by a small lamp on the desk. Adorning the walls are various military pictures, banners and insignia. This is the working office of a professional soldier. You head around the side of the desk and look at the desk top.

It's scrupulously neat and there's nothing of interest - only quills and ink and a few documents - nothing of interest, but requests for leave, uniform and acquisitions. You try the desk drawer, but it's locked.

Do you want to try to pick the lock?

If so, turn to **56**, if you would rather leave and try the other door, turn to **98**, or if you would prefer to go upstairs, turn to **50**

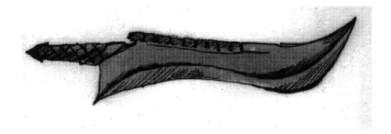

## 79

The chamber widens a bit and on both sides of the walls there are alcoves that reach from floor to ceiling. As you approach the first, you see that in the alcoves are standing skeletons of men long dead. Each skeleton has a shield in one arm and a sword in the other. You assume these were notable citizens of the city at some stage, as the tattered remnants of their clothing is fine. In the centre is one taller skeleton, in a fine robe that has stayed the effect of time. He has no shield, but instead held loosely in both hands is a large sword. The alcove around him is decorated with bleached white skulls. He was obviously a man of some importance, possibly a mighty warrior from an eon ago.

You reach up and touch the blade of the sword, but it is rusted beyond use.

Their resting place has now been used to expand the sewage system of the Holy City. You can almost feel their blank eyes following you as you try to creep past. Then you are past them and you breathe a sigh of relief. You are at another crossroads - and need to decide which way you are going to go now. Turn to **102**

## 80

Your hand reaches up when you are 10 foot off the ground and you put your cat's claws into the next brick, and move so that this hand primarily holds your weight. But then the old mortar crumbles, and without a chance to stop yourself, you fall to the floor, where you are stunned. Lose 2 **ENDURANCE** points.

The noise alerts even the laxest guards, and two come over to check. They can see the cat's claws glistening in the torch light on your hands and they curse. If you had escaped, it would have been their heads. Before you know it, the grate is open, and a long steel ladder lowered down. Two guards descend. If you have the **SKILL of UNARMED COMBAT**, you can try to use this but you must fight them together. As you have no weapons, reduce your **FIGHTING SKILL** by 2.

**GUARD 1**     **FIGHTING SKILL 6**     **ENDURANCE 5**
**GUARD 2**     **FIGHTING SKILL 7**     **ENDURANCE 6**

If you win, turn to **82**.

If your **ENDURANCE** gets to 2, they quickly overpower you, blindfold you and chain you to the walls using metal cuffs that cover the whole of the hands and don't leave your fingers free. There is no hope for escape now.

Turn to **13**

# 81

On the way out, you grab Jac from where you left him in Cell 2 recovering and you both leave as fast as you can.

Turn to **41**

# 82

You finally manage to knock the second guard unconscious with a swift side kick to the temple. You give each an extra blow across the head to ensure they sleep for many hours. You gasp for breath, but don't have any time to waste. Despite the pain and damage to your body you climb the ladder and haul yourself over the side of the oubliette. You pull up the ladder and close and lock the grate.

If you have the **SKILL of LOCK PICKING**, you can jam the lock so that the guards cannot escape, even though they have the keys.

If you do, turn to **12**

If not, turn to **60**

# 83

You notice a war banner hanging on one of the ground floor walls. It covers the wall completely from top to bottom. You initially missed it as it's such a dark area and not lit, but as you approach you can see footprints that have walked up to this banner, and seemingly through it. You approach carefully and pull the banner to one side.

**TEST YOUR FORTUNE and AGILITY**
Add both together and then roll 4d6. If you roll less than or equal to your total, turn to **99**. If you roll higher, turn to **10**

# 84

You edge towards the coffin, doubting yourself as you are going against all your better instincts. But it also feels like something you must do.

You brace yourself, and ready a stiletto, as you slowly reach over and unclip the hasp. You throw the lid back. Inside is a body.

It appears to be human – although initially it's difficult to tell. It's a woman, naked except for a white linen shift – at least you think it was probably once white. The whole of the material is drenched in blood. The bare arms, legs and head of the poor wretch are covered in puncture wounds from the spikes- dark black angry welts. As the spikes are barbed, this has the effect of ripping the flesh when the coffin is turned.

Having lived in Laeveni all your live, you are accustomed to seeing acts of violence and horror on an almost daily basis – but this is something else. You feel sick to your stomach. You decide to leave but just as you turn your back you hear a noise – a terrible empty moan. You can either:

Run! Turn to **69**
Or do you steel yourself and turn back. Turn to **45**

## 85

You pick up the iron keys. Make sure you note them on your adventure sheet. If you haven't already done so, you can now:

Search the bureau and shelves for anything useful, turn to **61**
Leave the room and try the large wood door, turn to **71**
Leave the room and walk down the corridor, turn to **74**

# 86

As a thief you still have the ability to try to pick a lock, but there is no guarantee you will manage. However, this is a large, basic lock and you should be able to open it. **TEST YOUR INTELLIGENCE**. If you roll less than or equal to your **INTELLIGENCE**, turn to **14**

If you roll more than your **INTELLIGENCE**, you struggle on trying to pick the lock but to no avail. Time suspended below the grate in the chimney of the oubliette saps your strength. Whilst you are trying one more time to open the lock, your leg cramps, causing you to slip. You fall to the ground of the oubliette with a thud.

Turn to **80**

# 87

Is Jac still alive?
If he is, turn to **31**
If he's not, turn to **25**

# 88

The lock gives way easily under your skilled touch. You hear a click as the locking mechanism releases. Nervous of the trap at the door, you stand to one side and slowly pull the draw open. Your care is rewarded, as there's a *"pfft"* sound and a small dart thuds into the leather back of the chair.

Using a pair of tweezers from your kit, you pluck the dart from the chair back and look closely at it. The point still glistens with a pale milky white liquid. You sniff the dart and smell nothing- as you suspected, d'cane poison. Lethal even in such small amounts. You look under the desk and find a hidden slot the towards the rear. You stick the point of one of your knives into it and you hear a *"clunk"* as the mechanism is deactivated.

You open the drawer with more confidence, and inside is a sheaf of papers. You rifle through them and stop suddenly, not believing your luck.

One of the papers is folded up but has the crest of Most Holy on it. You open it out and it is as you suspected, a map of the Holy City itself, listing all the guard placements and duties. This map if worth a fortune to a thief – if you can escape alive.

Smiling briefly, you stow the map in your tunic, replace all the other papers and close the drawer. Finally, you retrieve your knife and hear a *"tek"* as the mechanism resets. Record the map on your adventure sheet and gain **2 FORTUNE** points for such a good find. You leave the room.

Turn to **58**

## 89

The door creaks open. You slip through the door and swiftly and silently close it and turn around, but as you do you hear a noise like a taut wire snapping.

**TEST YOUR FORTUNE**.

If you have the **SKILL OF SPEED AND AGILITY** you can reduce the die roll by 2.

If you are lucky, turn to **39**.
If you are unlucky, turn to **57**

## 90

You find a smaller key on the key-chain, and first unlock the manacles on his legs. Then you reach up and unlock the manacles on his wrist and the man drops unceremoniously into a heap on the floor. Instantly you sense something is wrong and then you realise - the cage is made of silver – a valuable metal and known to have power over the undead.

But too late, as with preternatural speed the wretch springs up from the floor, a dreadful hunger in his eyes. Before your eyes he transforms into a spirit like creature, dressed in rags and he seems to float across the floor. He grabs you with talon like fingers. Before you can react, his vice like grip forces you to your knees and he bends his open mouth towards your neck.

The last thing you feel is the fetid breath from his mouth, which stinks of the grave and worse, and you sense more than see the glint of his unnaturally long, ragged teeth. Then you know no more as razor sharp incisors rip your throat out, and the Wight feasts noisily on you blood and flesh. Why a Wight is chained up in a simple guardroom you will never know, bound by silver that has power over its kind.

If you are fortunate, that'll be the end of you. If you are unlucky, then you may rise again to become a lesser Wight, doomed to spend eternity with only one thought in your mind – to feed on human flesh. Either way, your promising career as a thief ends here. You will be just another thief who never returns.

## 91

The gate creaks open. Beyond it is a short flight of stairs and as you walk up them, the stench of the room behind hits you full in the face. You live in a city by the sea, and are used to the smell of tanneries, breweries, fisheries, but this is the stench of human misery.

A combination of sweat, effluence and ammonia fill your nose. You fight down the reflex to retch. You calm your mind and try breathing through your mouth, but this just coats the inside of your mouth with a miasma so vile that you can almost taste the wretchedness in the room.

You carry on into the room. It's a long dark corridor, and on one side are a couple of dim torches giving off a ruddy orange glow as well as thick black smoke. On the other side are a number of cells, each with an iron gate.

Will you?
Open Cell 1? Turn to **66**
Open Cell 2? Turn to **53**
Open Cell 3? Turn to **47**
Open Cell 4? Turn to **49**
Open Cell 5? Turn to **100**

You cannot stand the feeling of having your arm in this hole for any longer and so you pull it out as quickly as you can. However, as you do, you disturb something and you feel a tiny nip on the back of your hand. You pull your hand out and look down. There are two small pin pricks in the back of your hand. Both are bleeding but what's more alarming is that the skin around the wound is swelling and turning green.

You watch in horror as this infection spreads up your arm, and you can feel it in your chest cavity. Your heart starts to beat three times its normal speed, and your breathing becomes fast and shallow, like a mutt panting. You feel tears running from your eyes and you try to rub them so they don't cloud your vision, but then everything takes on a red hue. You look down and your hands are covered in blood - your blood - which you realise is weeping freely from your eyes, nose and ears and elsewhere. You lurch forwards against the wall and wail once as your heart, overcome by the mysterious toxin, mercifully puts the end to your torment and explodes in your chest. You slump to the floor.

Your promising career as a thief ends here

Before you leave, you check the guard's pockets and find a set of iron keys. Then you go through the door and into a corridor. To the left, several yards away, there is a doorway that is just ajar and you can hear the noise of several men talking and laughing. You think it must be a common room for the off duty City Watch. Knowing that you do not have the strength or ability to take on this many foes, you discount this route. The room appears too bright for you to try to sneak through, even if you use arcane means.

To your right is another stout door. You try the keys. Turn to **89**

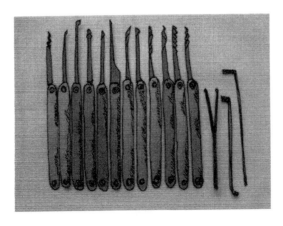

## 94

You are armed with both your stilettos against 2 guards armed with cudgels. You must fight them both together, and can only injure one guard per attack round, even if your **FIGHTING SKILL** roll is higher.

**GUARD 1    FIGHTING SKILL 8   ENDURANCE 9**
**GUARD 2    FIGHTING SKILL 7   ENDURANCE 8**

If your **ENDURANCE** gets down to 2 or less, turn to **28**. If you kill them both, turn to **61**

## 95

Jac and the beggar have not been idle whilst you fight the guard. Jac has wedged the door open, and then retrieved the paralysed guards cudgel and the beggar a length of chain. The beggar manages to throw the chain around the guard's cudgel and stop him from striking you whilst Jac hails down blow upon blow with the cudgel to the guard's head and body. Despite Jac's weakness, his blows help to down the guard. He is soon unconscious on the ground.

Turn to **5**

## 96

Too slow. You are still only halfway across the room. The first watchman, who is standing holding the door open, shouts *"Oi, you, stop"*

You have nowhere to go, and are outnumbered 2 to 1.

Do you have the **SKILL** of **CHARM AND GUILE**. If so, turn to **52** If you don't, turn to **44**

## 97

You leave, locking the cell door as you exit. If you haven't already, will you?

Open Cell 2? Turn to **53**
Open Cell 3? Turn to **47**
Open Cell 4? Turn to **49**
Open Cell 5? Turn to **100**

## 98

You warily approach the right hand door, and examine the door frame and handle. Nothing appears out of the ordinary and so you turn the handle and open it. The door creaks slightly, a noise that is magnified in the quiet of the tower. In front of you is a kitchen area. You look around and find enough provisions for 4 meals. Add them to your adventure sheet. You also find a small potion bottle. It's a potion of **FORTUNE** that can increase your **FORTUNE** by one point (even above initial levels) but for one **FORTUNE** test only - so use it sparingly. Add this to your adventure sheet. You leave the room and are back in the hallway.

Turn to **42**

# 99

You hear a slight click as you pull the banner to one side. In a movement made out of instinct and not thought, you dive and roll to one side. Just in time as a something fizzes past where your head was moments ago. You recover to your feet in one fluid move and see something shiny stuck into the opposite wall. You sneak over and check. It's a small metal dart, no doubt tipped with poison.

You shrug, and walk back to the wall hanging and find the hidden trigger. Having disabled the trap, you walk into a small alcove. There are no doors from it, but on the floor is a metal grate.

Turn to **109**

# 100

This cell has been converted into a temporary storeroom. The cell door in unlocked, and you ease the door open. The room is littered with junk. Barrels of ale for the guards, piles of clothes, bags and other garments. There's a chest in the corner that's got a simple hasp lock on it.

Do you want to search the room? If so, turn to **59**

If not, you leave. If you haven't already done so you can check the other cells.

Open Cell 1? Turn to **66**
Open Cell 2? Turn to **53**
Open Cell 3? Turn to **47**
Open Cell 4? Turn to **49**

# 101

You choose left and continue along a short corridor that takes a sudden right turn. The light continues to fade as you get deeper into the oldest parts of the city. You feel like you are slowly going downhill and the air is getting thicker and distinctly unpleasant.

The whole area smells of a combination of damp, must and decay. You think you half hear a sort of scuttling noise ahead but there's nothing visible. You arrive at another crossroads.

You have three choices – left, right or straight on. The corridor to the left is dark and the air is still, but it doesn't seem to go on for long. The one in front of you just seems long and straight but you cannot determine anything else. To the right, the corridor seems to become more ornate, with stone columns and plinths. It seems to be an even older part of the catacombs.

Do you want to go left, turn to **118**, straight on, turn to **111**, or right, turn to **145**

## 102

You stand there at the crossroads considering the best route to take. Then all of a sudden you hear a clattering noise behind you, and then the clank of metal on metal. You turn quickly and are horrified to see that the skeletons are emerging from their alcoves, their shields before them and their swords levelled and pointed towards your heart. You are going to have to fight them. Throw 1d6, this is how many skeletons you must face.

You draw your sword and prepare to face the reanimated creatures.

**SKELETONS**          **FIGHTING SKILL 8   ENDURANCE 6**

Luckily as the corridor has narrowed once more they can only engage you one at a time. If you win, turn to **131**

## 103

You arrive at yet another junction. It's a crossroads but you think that you have already been down the right tunnel, and so you can ignore that way. The passage to the left seems to drop down even further into the earth. It's steep, and earthy. There is a slight breeze from the tunnel, but it brings the smell of decadence and decay. The route straight on is a tunnel constructed of stone bricks, aged with time.

To go straight on, turn to **148**. To go left, turn to **75**

## 104

The rate of decent is making it difficult for you to keep on your feet, and you half scramble down the passageway until you get to a point where it levels out - and you realise that all your effort was a waste - as in front of you is a dead end.

You have no choice but to try to scramble back up the incline, but in doing so you cut yourself badly on a sharp of volcanic glass that is sticking out from the passageway floor. Lose 2 **ENDURANCE**. You get back to the top, and have no option but to go down the other passage.

Turn to **146**

## 105

This subterranean network is like a rabbit warren. Every few yards you come to another junction - and once again you find yourself having to choose. You are finding it increasingly difficult to keep track of your whereabouts in this almost alien landscape. You look at the next junction, and see again you can turn left or right, or carry straight on.

The left passage is composed of large bricks that seem to be loose, with little or no mortar to hold them in place. The right passage is strewn with boulders on the floor, which will make it difficult to negotiate. Straight on, the passage appears to have a warm breeze.

If you dare to go left, turn to **141**. If you think right is the best way, turn to **136.** Or to go straight, turn to **122**

## 106

You reach into your backpack and your hand finds the **DEATH SIGIL** given to you by Inista in her last moments. It is a powerful curse. You clench your fist around it, and then extend your arm. De-Villiers is overly eager, and reaches out for your hand. You open your fist, and drop the **SIGIL** into his hand.

Turn to **117**

## 107

*"Ah, we have a rabbit. A quick rabbit, but I am quicker. I am the hawk, who catches the rabbit"* shouts Celdron as he darts his blade towards you. The thin point pierces your side and into your heart. You drop to the floor. Before you die, you hear the sound of a fist striking flesh, and a cry of pain from Celdron.

*"Celdron, you fool, you were too quick, I wanted him taken alive, to question in cells. Still, this is the one I was looking for, and hopefully he still has the token I require. You had better hope he has, or I will take you to the cell below, and you will know torment"*

Your death is fortunate in that it is quick. Your promising career as a thief ends here.

## 108

De-Villiers is too strong and skillful and after a valiant effort, you drop to your knees in exhaustion. You raise your blade weakly to try to stop the next blow, but De-Villiers simply slaps it from your weakening grip with the flat of his sword. He smiles, almost fatherly, down at you.

**"Brave, brave boy"** he says **"My Master can make use of a servant like you"** and he raises his hand and brings down the black glass knife into your shoulder, but only gently.

The blade is so sharp you do not feel it enter, but then De-Villiers twists the blade and removes it from you. You can see a tiny shard of the blade has chipped off the point, and you can feel it's coldness in your body. Then you watch in amazement as the knife repairs itself.

**"Not long now my brave boy, and you will become a servant to My Master. You kept the last key to his prison from him, and so I doubt he will be a kindly master to you - but you will grow to both fear and love him over the millennia. You will never die, you will never grow old, never be sick - but you will also never be alive again."**

And he turns his back and walks off. Your body feels a dread cold as the sliver of the glass blade works its way to your heart, and then you don't feel again as your life ebbs away and you start a new existence undead forever, as a wraith in the service of De-Villiers unnamed master.

Your promising career as a thief ends here.

## 109

You crouch down and check the grate. It's made of wrought iron, but badly rusted. You heave at it but it's not shifting. But scuff marks indicate that is has recently been opened. You are sure this is the way to go and so don't want to stop. Perhaps there is another way to open it. You look around the alcove.

**TEST YOUR FORTUNE**.

If you have the **SKILL of SIXTH SENSE**, you can take 2 off the roll and not lose a **FORTUNE** point if you win. If you don't have this skill, roll as usual.
If you are **FORTUNATE**, turn to **119**. If you are not, turn to **130**

Another tunnel leads off downhill, leading into the dark. The walls of the corridor are thick stone not earth, but there are cracks in the roof of the tunnel. You hold your nerve and carry on down into the dark. Then all of a sudden you hear a deep rumbling in the earth, and the ground starts to shake. You cannot keep on your feet; such is the violence of the upheaval. You are knocked onto your back, and with horror you see that about you the roof and sides of the tunnel are shaking and cracking.

You scramble back up, to run back up the tunnel, but stone dust and earth streams down from the roof onto your head, making it impossible to see where you are going. Disorientated, you try to feel your way back up. But then the earth is replaced by rocks that become dislodged and rubble starts to rain down on you, hitting your head, shoulders and back. You double over to try to protect yourself from this deluge.

But then the rock fall dislodges some larger boulders and one about the size of a dwarf falls on top of you and crushes your slender body. Soon your battered remains are completely buried under an impromptu stone cairn, which will hold your broken form until the end of time. Your promising career as a thief ends here

## *111*

You turn into a long vaulted tunnel that smells of damp, decay and something almost alien. Then you hear a scuttling all around you and you draw back when you see long forms scuttling towards you. Each is about 3 yards long, and with hundreds of short legs on each side of its long, low body.

These legs propel their long bodies' forwards in a smooth scurrying motion. Their bodies are segmented and covered in hard chitin, the outer shell of insects. Their eyes are very small as they are almost blind, but on the front of their heads are long antenna that constantly feel and taste the air. They sense you, as their large mandibles click together in anger. You have disturbed a nest of giant centipedes and you have no choice but to fight them. Throw 1d6 to determine how many you have to fight.

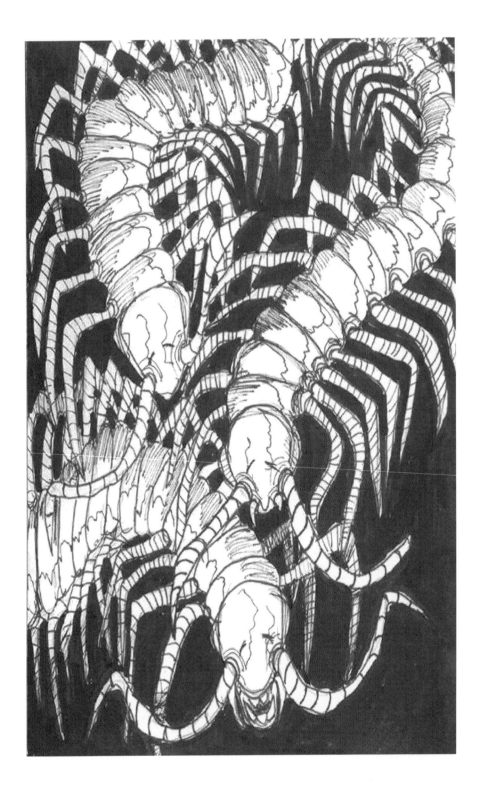

**GIANT CENTIPEDES**          **FIGHTING SKILL 8   ENDURANCE 7**

If you win turn to **7**

Otherwise your promising career as a thief ends here, as a meal for the young in their nest.

## 112

You deliver a final blow to the ethereal form of De-Villiers, and he screams out

**"My Lord, why have you forsaken me. You promised me life eternal."**

Deep in those eyes you can see anger and contempt, but also fear and a begrudging respect for you - as you, a mere gutter rat, have defeated him. Then he says in a voice as quiet as death

**"But you are too late. All the keys are near now. My master stirs even now and others will do his bidding. You face oblivion, fool"**

His form explodes in a flash of light, but there is no noise, but there is a terrific rush of air. You turn and run fast, as you can sense a malevolent presence in the chamber.

You run as fast as you can up the passageway near the altar. You feel something gathering behind you but dare not look back. You sprint to the surface.

Turn to **150**

## 113

The climb down the ladder is no more than 10 feet. You drop down and land lightly to the floor below, dropping into a crouch with your hands on your dagger hilts. The ground is hard and smooth and part of the extensive sewers. Somewhere under here you hope is an exit back into the city. The passage is dark and so you look around and find what you think is a long stick. You pick it up and realise that it is in fact the thigh bone of a man. You shudder. You wrap some rags around it and light it with your flint. It shows the path ahead, dropping down deeper into the bowels of the sewers. You follow the corridor straight on until you come to a crossroads.

The way right is blocked by a rock fall. There is a path to the left or you can continue straight on. As you approach the left passage, your torch starts to splutter. When you check the straight passageway, you can feel a warmth from the entrance.

If you want to turn left, turn to **128**. To continue on the straight path, turn to **122**

## *114*

Despite his skill and double attack, you manage to finally cut De-Villiers down with a deft backhand slice to his throat. The fighting you have had to do so far tonight has sharpened your skills beyond what they once were. His eyes go wide in disbelief as his life's blood starts to flood out of the gaping hole in his neck.

He drops to his knees gasping and cursing you - although you can hardly make out a word he is saying as he chokes on his own blood. The knife and sword fall from his hands as he grasps his throat in a desperate attempt to stem the blood flow. As the knife drops to the hard stone floor, it shatters into a thousand pieces leaving only the rune carved hilt behind. As it breaks there is a silent detonation as the malevolent energy stored in the knife escapes.

Then De-Villiers topples to one side and his body starts to rapidly decompose, as though the work of ages happens in seconds. Soon there is nothing left but dust, which blows away in an unnatural gust of a witch wind.

You rest a while and feel replenished – add 4 to your **ENDURANCE** - and then start to look around the chamber. You find to the left of the dark altar a passageway leading steeply up. Then just as you are about to take it and leave this ungodly room, an unholy wind whistles through the chamber, stirring up dust that forms into a whirlwind in the centre of the room, buffeting you.

Then the whirlwind slowly turns into an ethereal human form of a very old man, but it's still a face that you know - the face of the man you have just defeated! He is wearing a shimmering unearthly robe and his long hair is intricately braided. The figures hovers' unerringly in front of you and it seems to carry the stench of decadence, decay and evil. In his pale hand he holds a white sword seemingly made of smoke.

He throws back his head and laughs, a dusty and cold sound that echoes through the remnants of this great city.

*"You fool; you think you could defeat me so easily. You just destroyed the corporal form that my Master granted me for this oh so important task. Now you see my true form. For too long, I have waited in the cold ground for my Master to give me the strength to bring him back to your world, his world.*

*He returns! Can you not feel it? And the world will tremble as He wakes. And you have brought the final tools I need to resurrect Him. And I will be the most esteemed of all His servants. Now give me what I want, or I shall take it"*
Turn to **126**

## 115

You are starting to get increasingly confused by the layout of these corridors, and again you end up at a junction whereby you can turn left or right. You check your bearings and consider your options. The tunnel to the right heads downhill, and the walls are made from stone bricks. You look up and the roof is cracked.

To go right, turn to **110**. Otherwise, turn to **141**

## 116

The corridor, if it can be called that, narrows as you walk through it until your arms are brushing the walls, and then it comes to a dead end. On the floor is some debris including a small glass bottle. If you want to pick up the bottle, turn to **125**.

Otherwise there is no way through here and you must turn around and walk back up the corridor and take the other passage.

Turn to **105**

## 117

The Sigil glows red in his De-Villiers hand. The star in the centre radiates an ethereal light. He screams, an unearthly sound that comes from no human throat. He tries to drop the Sigil, but his muscles seem to have contracted and hold his fist closed around it. You see smoke appear from his clenched fist, and smell the charnel reek of burning flesh. A dark fire starts in his clasped hand, and starts to travel up his arm.

He screams, sounding more like a terrified child, but the fire continues to climb. Soon he is engulfed in it, and he burns with black flames. His flesh starts to crumble from his bones, and soon he is just a charred skeleton. He topples to the floor, and his bones shatter on impact with the ground, leaving a heap of dust and bone fragments.

You hear a female voice in your head *"It is done, I have my revenge"* and then it's gone.

The Sigil remains glowing in the dust but then the colour starts to leave it, until it looks once more just like a harmless trinket. You reach down and pick it up. It's hot to the touch and you burn your hand. Lose 1 **ENDURANCE**. But you wait for it to cool and put it back into your pack.

Not wanting to waste any more time, you head for the passageway behind the altar and head for the surface.
Turn to **143**

## 118

The corridor is short and goes back on itself into a dead end. On the floor, covered in dust is a skeleton of a man, still clad in a rusty mail coat. If you want to examine the skeleton, turn to **33**.

Otherwise you can return to the junction and go straight on, turn to **145**, or turn left, turn to **111**

## 119

Searching around you notice there is an unevenness about the wall - one that does not appear to be from disrepair. You trace you hand along the rough uneven stones, and then sense that one of them feels slightly different. You place your knife into one of the edges. You slowly twist and the stone pivots open on a hinge.

Behind the stone is a small hole that goes back into the wall. You peer in and can see only blackness. You take a chance and place you hand and forearm into the hole and reach back. You flinch as something runs over the back of your hand. Then a second something does as well.

Do you want to slowly consider probing the hole, then turn to **121**, or quickly remove your arm, turn to **92**

## 120

Your hand closes on the amulet. As it touches your hand, you remember all the horror you have seen tonight and feel rage that this man has been the source of it. But you feel the resistance in you failing, as De-Villiers almost hypnotic voice continues to persuade you.

**TEST YOUR FORTUNE**. If you pass, turn to **142**
If you fail, turn to **133**

## 121

You decide not to startle whatever is in there and move slowly and continue to probe with your hand. The scurrying of tiny feet across your hand continues and you steel yourself so you don't inadvertently flinch and startle whatever's in there.

Eventually, after hours, in reality mere moments, of searching your hand finds something sticking up. A lever! You slowly pull it and are rewarded by a squeal of rust and iron as the hidden mechanism releases the grate. It slowly creaks open. With all care, you slowly inch your hand out of the opening and eventually pull it free.

On the back of your hand is a tiny red beetle, with over enlarged mandibles. You place your hand back onto the wall near the hole and it scuttles off your hand back into its home.

Turn to **138**

## 122

The corridor continues to slope downward as you walk along it, and the air gets a mustier smell about it and it's oppressively warm. You start to sweat profusely in the close atmospheres, exacerbated by your need to carry a lit torch. You carry on without incident for about 200 yards and then come to a crossroads.

If you want to turn left, turn to **101**. If you want to turn right, turn to **147**, or if you would prefer to go straight on, turn to **127**

## 123

You rest a while and feel replenished – add 4 to your **ENDURANCE** - and then start to look around the chamber. You find to the left of the dark altar a passageway leading steeply up. Then just as you are about to take it and leave this ungodly room, an unholy wind whistles through the chamber, bringing dust that forms a whirlwind in the centre of the room, buffeting you with the wind.

Then the whirlwind slowly turns into an ethereal human form of a very old man, but it's still a face that you know - the face of the man you have just defeated! He is wearing a shimmering unearthly robe and his long hair is intricately braided. The figures hovers' unerringly in front of you and it seems to carry the stench of decadence, decay and evil. In his pale hand he holds a white sword seemingly made of smoke.

He throws back his head and laughs, a dusty and cold sound that echoes through the remnants of this great city.

*"You fool; you think you could defeat me so easily. You just destroyed the corporal form that my Master granted me for this oh so important task. Now you see my true form. For too long, I have waited in the cold ground for my Master to give me the strength to bring him back to your world, his world.*

*He returns! Can you not feel it? And the world will tremble as He wakes. And you have brought the final tools I need to resurrect him. And I will be the most esteemed of all His servants. Now give me what I want, or I shall take it"*

**TEST YOUR FORTUNE**
If you are **FORTUNATE**, turn to **4**
If you are not, turn to **126**

De-Villiers walks into the room and surveys it. He notices the trap has been tripped and he says to himself.

**"Tripped, but no body. Someone is here. In this room"**

He has not seen you but somehow he feels your presence and remains in the centre of the room. His eyes search the room intently. Then, without turning, he shouts. The door opens almost immediately, and two men wearing the uniform of the Black Guard appear.

One is small, slight and moves quickly. His hair is greasy and seemingly plastered to his head and face, as well as a scraggly beard covering most of his pock marked face. This is a face not to trust. His dark eyes glitter cruelly under his brows. Celdron! One of De-Villiers most trusted Lieutenants. What he lacks in size he makes up for in viciousness.

The other is the opposite. Tall and broad, but without enough bulk to slow him down. He towers above Celdron, and a broad headed battle axe is hooked into his belt. His hair is long, blonde and braided, and his face clean-shaven. It would be a friendly, attractive face if it wasn't for his eyes, which shine like blue ice – but there is no emotion in these eyes.

This is Elrad, Celdron's normal accomplice when working for De-Villiers. He is the brawn to Celdrons brains – and he enjoys using his brawn.

**"Search the tower"** instructs De-Villiers **"someone has entered. And still lives"**

They fan out, with Celdron moving the closest to you. You realise your poor hiding place will soon be found and you have no choice but to make a run for it. You dart for the door, but as fast as you are, Celdron is faster. His rapier whistles from his scabbard and he strikes at you as you fly past.

**TEST YOUR FORTUNE**. If you are fortunate, turn to **107**. If you are not, turn to **19**

# 125

The bottle is dusty and covered with dirt from the ground, but you give it a quick clean and see a run on the side that identifies it as a **POTION of ENDURANCE**. This potion will restore your endurance to its original level, but use it wisely as there is only one dose. Write this on your adventure sheet, and now you must go back up the tunnel.

Turn to **105**

# 126

You are held by his voice, which commands you to remain. But in a show of defiance, you once more raise your weapons. You may not be able to run, but you will fight.

*"Heh heh heh. So you still wish to fight. You still think you can beat me. You may have beaten my physical form, but you will find me a lot harder to destroy now. It is inconceivable that you will defeat me"*

He moves towards you.

**SPIRIT of DE-VILLIERS     FIGHTING SKILL 13 ENDURANCE 23**

He is not of this earth and cannot be easily harmed. If you hit him, roll 1d6. If you roll a 5 or a 6, your attack fails. Each successful attack from him is also magical and as well as hurts you physically, you lose 1 point of **FIGHTING SKILL** as well as **2 ENDURANCE**.

If you win, turn to **112**

# 127

The tunnel continues to go downward and the air is stifling and thick. It's like trying to breathe through a wet blanket and the moisture causes you to struggle to catch your breath. Lose 2 **ENDURANCE**.

Eventually, you come to a left turn, and the air seems even thicker down that route. The tunnel to the right seems larger and more open, with a higher, arched roof. The walls are made of tight fitting bricks and you can see in the gloom a couple of carved stone columns rising up to the roof.

Do you want to turn left, if so turn to **145**. Otherwise you carry on straight, turn to **79**

# 128

You take the left turn and again the path starts to go steeply downhill. It continues to be as dark as the pits of hell here, but your torch gives you some light. Then your torch starts to splutter and the flame slowly decreases in size almost like the fire is slowly suffocating. Then all of a sudden the flame is extinguished and you are plunged into almost total darkness. You try not to panic, as you are used to operating in the dark, but not underground on the way to an ancient city to fight a terrible foe. You rely on your other senses, as you have done on many a time.

It's then that you notice a thick acrid smell in the tunnel. It gets stronger with every step and it when you inhale it, the acrid stench bites the back of your throat making you cough uncontrollably. The more you cough, the more you breathe in and the less you can breathe. Soon you are half coughing and half panting, leaning against the tunnel walls. Your head spins with lack of oxygen and the build-up of toxic gas.

Too late you realise that you are in a pocket of marsh gas but by then the gas has done its deadly work. You gasp once more, your eyes now streaming from the toxin, and slump to the floor. Your last few breathes in this life are shallow and rasping. Then you breathe no more.

Your promising career as a thief ends here

# 129

You reach down and close her eyes, but as you do her head jerks to one side, and you realise she's only mostly dead. Some life still remains in her.

But she starts to fade. But before she does she weakly raises her hand and presses an item into your hand. Its round, with a star in the centre and compelling symbols around the star. Around the edge are letters, possibly spelling a name, but you cannot make it out: A…R..O..T..H..A..S..T. The star glows with a feint light.

*"This is my amulet. It contains my Sigil of power. It connects me to…… the one from my eternal master…..from whom I….. draw my power. I have placed upon it my …….death curse…………. for the man who did this to me. This may aide you in destroying him, for he is more than……. He seems, for he is…….."*

She coughs and struggles to speak. You lean in even closer as its clear there is something important she needs to tell you.

*"De….vil…."* she whispers in a voice like dry parchment.

Then her head drops to one side, and you hear the rattle of the air leaving her body for the last time. You close her eyes and pray that she finds peace. Then you think you see an ethereal human shape leaving her and floating above her body. The face then comes into focus, and you see the face of an impossibly beautiful young woman, with long silken hair, looking down at you and smiling.

Her smile fills you with joy and hope. Add 1 to your **FORTUNE** and **FIGHTING SKILL** (even if either exceeds 12). You feel blessed and tears fill your eyes. But then she is gone.

You stand and walk towards the cell door. Remember to put **SIGIL OF DEATH** onto your adventure sheet.

Turn to **41**

## 130

You cannot find a way to open the grate and despite heaving at it, you cannot shift it. Lose 1 **FORTUNE** point. You have no choice but to try to sneak back out the main door.

Turn to **132**

## 131

Your blade chops the head clean from the last skeleton. It bounces along the stone floor, and cracks into pieces. The body remains standing for a moment, its arms still twitching for a few seconds. Then it collapses to the ground into a pile of dust and bones. For fighting well, gain 1 **FORTUNE** point.

Having sent the skeletons back to their graves, you can continue. You come to another crossroads. You crouch down and examine the various paths. You fancy you can see vague footprints in the dust heading straight on, but you cannot tell how recent they are. The floor of the right tunnel is covered with dust and does not seem to have been disturbed for decades. You cannot determine anything of use from the left passage.

At the crossroads are you going to turn left (turn to **103**), turn right (turn to **148**) or go straight on (turn to **75**)

## 132

As you head back to the door, you hear a click, and then you see it start to open. In desperation, you hide back in the shadows. The door opens and a tall, thin, sardonic man enters. He is wearing the insignia of a Kaptain of the Guard. You recognise his face. It's De-Villiers himself.

You remain still, just backed against a wall, hoping the shadows and your dark clothes hide you. You are crouched down to make your profile as small as possible, and you lower your head so that your dark hair covers your pale face. You stare up through your hair with eyes like slits.

**TEST YOUR FORTUNE.** If you have **the SKILL OF HIDING IN SHADOWS**, you can take 2 off your roll.

If you pass, turn to **144**. If you fail, turn to **124**

## 133

You feel your will crumbling under the onslaught of the mind of De-Villiers. He seems to have power over your body and with horror you see your hand going to your backpack and taking out the red stone. You hold out your hand and he slowly walks forward, his face a mask of triumph, and snatches the contents from your hand.

**"At least"** he shouts **"I have them all. The keys to release the greatest power this world has known. It has taken many millennia, but I will now free Him and be His most favoured right hand. And you, boy, will serve Him for eternity. But as you tried to go against his wishes, I doubt you will find Him a kindly master".**

You have failed to stop the ancient power emerging, and soon it will take over all of your world, and you will be there to see all the horror and terror to come.

Your promising career as a thief ends here

You turn left and continue down a long tunnel, but you can see some feint light at the end. You suppress the need to run towards the light as the darkness - which you were born to - is repressive in this underworld. Instead you hold your nerve and continue forward on cat like feet. Light at the end of the tunnel may mean further enemies.

The tunnel starts to broaden out a bit and you find yourselves at an ornately carved archway. You walk through the archway into a large chamber. Light cascades down from above from a hidden source far above. There is a waterfall passing through it, and the walls are all carved and painted - although the paint has blistered and peeled from the walls over time, or faded into obscurity.

On the other side of the chamber is a raised platform and elegant pillars rise up to the tall vaulted ceilings. At the rear of the chamber is an altar made of black basalt. The surface is old and pitted, and knife marks are clear on the surface. In the altar are channels which are stained dark - with what you aren't certain, until you smell a metallic scent rising from the altar.

You shudder. The altar is stained with blood that has turned dark over the ages. At the back of the altar is a statue of a creature made from nightmares - and you realise that this is the power that you are destined to fight.  Then a figure emerges out from behind a pillar and greets you. He is tall and sardonic and welcomes you with a thin smile. You know this face all too well.

Turn to **29**

# *135*

As you walk into the passageway you sense more than see that the roof of the passageway extends up like a chimney, the bricks old with age from some long lost structure. At the top you can see the vague hint of light as if there is a route out of this subterranean hell. You look up and strain your eyes to see more.

Then all of a sudden you see some small black forms flying around above you, circling high up in the chimney. Then all of a sudden as one they dive and attack you. You shudder as one of them tries to land on you and bite your neck with needle like fangs. They are vampire bats, and are keen to taste your blood. You must fight them. There are 4 bats,

**VAMPIRE BATS     FIGHTING SKILL 5   ENDURANCE 5**

You must fight them all at once. If you throw a double on the bats winning attack round, then one of the bats manages to attach itself to you and drains 3 **ENDURANCE** in blood.

If you succeed turn to **137**

Another tunnel leads off downhill, leading into the dark. The walls of the corridor are thick stone not earth, but there are cracks in the roof of the tunnel. You hold your nerve and carry on down into the dark. Then the corridor opens up into a large cavern. You enter between two ancient pillars and look at the almost perfectly round chamber which has a dome that reaches up for fully 50 yards.

Then all of a sudden you hear a deep rumbling in the earth, and the ground starts to shake. You cannot keep on your feet; such is the violence of the upheaval. You are knocked onto your back, and turn towards the noise - the corridor you enter through. With horror you see that about you the roof and sides of the tunnel are shaking and cracking and then the two stone pillars crash to the ground. Stone dust and earth streams down from the roof, which then changes to rubble, and then to boulders. The air becomes black with dust and you choke back breaths of air, taking in more dust than precious air.

Then as quickly as it started, the rock falls stops. You struggle to your feet, coughing up earth dust, and blindly feel around. Panic gets hold of your heart and for a few moments you stand there still, not knowing what to do. Then you compose yourself, with a struggle, and assess where you are. Behind you, the way you came in, 20 feet back the whole of the corridor has been filled with giant boulders that will be impossible for a cave troll to move, let alone a young thief.

You take time to examine the cavern. It looks like an old temple to some ancient god. But it appears that the only way in was through the carved pillars. Slowly, you realise that there is no way out and that you only have the time left that your provisions will provide.

You have two options. You can ration your food and hope that someone finds you, which seems unlikely as no one knows you are here, until you finally die of starvation, or more likely, thirst. Or you can take the easy way out. You draw your knife and look at its keen edge. It is so sharp you will barely feel the cut.

You must decide what you must do, but either way, your promising career as a thief ends here.

## 137

You stop and rest against the wall, breathing heavily, taking the time to staunch any blood flow from the bats bites, as their fangs inject an anticoagulant to keep you bleeding. If you have any guano, you can spread this on your wound, as you have heard that the soil from vampire bats will help against their bites.

If you do not have any guano, then you lose 2 **ENDURANCE** as you cannot get the bleeding to stop.

Turn to **139**

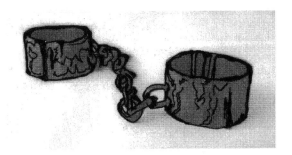

## 138

You look down at the grate and see it has opened halfway. You stamp with the heel of your boot and it protests as you force it open. The wail is almost like that of a human baby. Eventually you force it open all the way. You crouch down and look into the darkness, once more steadying your nerves. You sit on the edge and look down.

All is as quiet and as dark as a grave. You reach to the wall and find a bit of crumbled mortar and drop it down, listening intently. You hear it land scant seconds later and determine it must be more than 30 yards to the ground - or whatever is below.

You prepare yourself to climb down into the pit, but then half smile as you see a glitter of metal against one of the walls. There is a ladder bolted to the side of the tunnel. You gladly climb onto it and silently descend into the darkness. The grate swings closed with a rusty crash. You have no way out, and you must now carry on down into the unknown. Turn to **113**

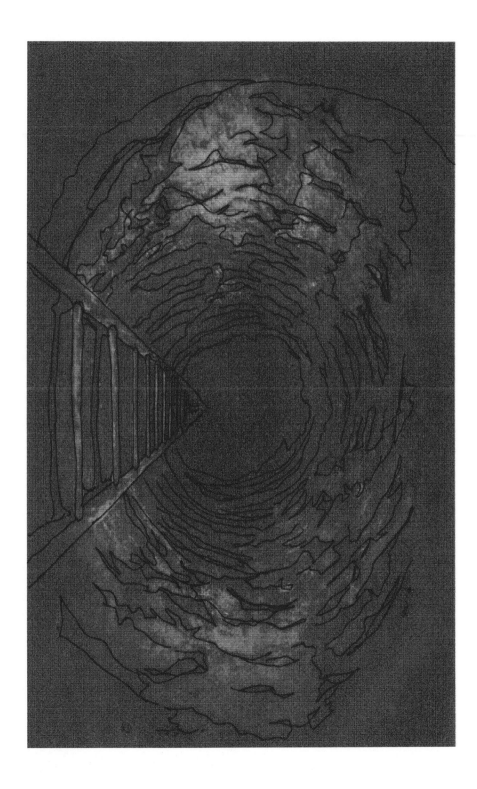

## 139

You continue along a corridor that descends quickly and now have the choice of whether to continue straight on or turn left. The passage straight on descends down steeply into the ground. You peer into the tunnel and cannot feel a breath of moving air, and the air smells stale.

The tunnel to the left also descends deeply, but you can feel a slight flow of air, carrying the smell of decay, but also something else. Something you are familiar with but cannot quite place.

Will you go straight on (turn to **104**) or turn left (turn to **146**)

## 140

You hide in the corner and you use all your training to become almost preternaturally still. You try to slow your breathing and are almost in a trance like state.

It seems to work as one of the guards goes into another room, whilst the other remains at the door. The first guard emerges with some sheaves of paper. Then they both leave the way they came, and the door locks behind them.

You decide you will have to see what's beyond the iron gate.

Turn to **91**

## 141

You have a bad feeling about the right hand tunnel, and so instead decide to go left. You soon end up at another junction. You feel like you have been here before. You worry that you are getting lost and turned around in this maze and you fight down the panic that's rising in your chest.

The tunnel to the left may be new, but you are struggling to tell. The one to the right is made of stone brick, with cracked walls and ceilings, and looks familiar. But you cannot wait any longer. You must choose.

Either go left, and turn to **115**, or choose right and turn to **110**

## 142

Your will is strong and you refuse to yield, thinking of the evil you have seen tonight. You shake your head and your hand moves away from your backpack and towards your sword hilt. De-Villiers mask of civility slips and his face clouds in rage.

***"You disobey me? You dare! I have passed eons waiting for this moment and will not be defeated. It is time for Him to rise again. If you will not give it to me, then I will take it"***

Then from inside his robe he draws a sable like blade and a short hooked knife of black glass. The knife is old with age but still looks razor sharp.

**DE-VILLIERS          FIGHTING SKILL 11  ENDURANCE 9**

Each time De-Villiers hits you, throw 1d6. If you throw even, then his sword hurts you and does the usual 2 **ENDURANCE** damage, but if it's odd, the knife hurts you. The knife is the sacrificial blade that has been used for centuries and has an evil power - and each cut from the knife does 3 **ENDURANCE** damage. If you win, turn to **114**. If you lose, turn to **108**

You have only just started back up the tunnel when you hear a noise from behind you. You stop and turn. You can see back in the chamber, where a whirlwind is forming around De-Villiers remains, and slowly turns into an ethereal human form of a very old man. He is wearing a shimmering unearthly robe and his long hair is intricately braided. Even from here, he seems to carry the stench of decadence, decay and evil. In his pale hand he holds a white sword seemingly made of smoke.

The figure floats across the chamber and looks at the passageway back up to the surface. It tests the air in front with its sword, but some sort of invisible field stops it. He cannot leave without a corporal body. He stares at you with glowing eyes.

However, the ghostly spectre throws back his head and laughs, a dusty and cold sound that echoes through the catacombs.

*"You fool; you think you could defeat me so easily. You just destroyed the corporal form that my Master granted me for this oh so important task. For too long, I have waited in the cold ground for my Master to give me the strength to bring him back to your world, His world. He returns! And the world will tremble as He wakes. I know you have the final tool I need to resurrect Him. And I will be the most esteemed of all His servants."*

Turn to **150**

## 144

De-Villiers walks into the room and surveys it. Then he says to himself **"The trap was tripped, but there is no body. Someone is here"**, closing the door behind him. You hear it click as he locks it.

**"Maybe he is below in the catacombs"** and he dashes towards a dark corner, where there is a war banner hanging.

He reaches around and you hear a switch "**click**" and he disappears behind the banner. You hear the sound of rusted metal protesting, and then steps echoing down below. Then the metal groans shut again.

Turn to **149**

## 145

Once again you arrive at a junction. You feel like you have been down the right corridor, although you could be mistaken. You bend down and check the floor, and you can see vague footprints. The imprint matches the soles of your boots, and so you are convinced that you have already been this way

Therefore, you have no option but to turn left. Your torch is starting to burn low and so you decide to hurry.

Turn to **79**

## 146

You half scramble down another steeply slanted passageway and when you get to the bottom there's a choice of turning left or right. You check both passages. The floor of the right passage is soft and sandy, and you struggle with your footing. The left passage seems much longer, but you think you can detect light at the end, but there is something about this passage that is deeply unsettling.

Do you want to turn left, then turn to **134**, or head right, and turn to turn to **35**

# 147

Shortly after turning right, you find yourself at another junction. The left hand passage heads downhill, into the dark and there is dust in the air that makes you cough. The right passage seems to get smaller as it goes on, but appears shorter.

You can either choose to turn right, then turn to **116**, otherwise turn left and turn to **136**

# 148

Another choice. You can either go straight on, or turn left. You examine the tunnel walls and notice the passage straight on is made of large, ill-fitting bricks and stones. The mortar has crumbled from between them with age. The left passage descends down, and has a musty smell to it, but a slight breeze that brings a whiff of tallow.

If you go straight on, turn to **110,** or to go left and turn to **75**

# 149

You wait for half an hour, but De-Villiers does not re-appear. You check the door, and behind it you hear the sound of many voices. The only way out is to try to follow De-Villiers.

You walk over to the war banner, and pull it to one side and walk back into the alcove.

You crouch down and check the grate again. It's still locked. You heave at it but it's not shifting. But you can see fresh scuff marks from when De-Villiers opened it. You are sure this is the way De-Villiers went and so perhaps there is another way to open it. You rack your brain. The noise you heard was not of a key being turned in a lock, but more like a catch being released. There must be a secret lever hidden in this alcove. With renewed belief, you check.

Searching around you notice there is an unevenness about the wall - one that does not appear to be from disrepair. You trace your hand along the rough uneven stones, and then sense that one of them feels slightly different. You place your knife into one of the edges. You slowly twist and the stone pivots open on a hinge.

Behind the stone is a small hole that goes back into the wall. You peer in and can see only blackness, although you think you saw something move. You take a chance and place you hand and forearm into the hole and reach back. You flinched as something runs over the back of your hand. Then a second something does as well.

Do you want to slowly consider probing the hole, then turn to **121**, or risk quickly removing your arm, turn to **92**

## *150*

As if the devil is on your back, you run as fast as you can up the steep tunnel, breathing heavily. It is large, fully 10 yards across, and twists and turns as it heads for the surface. The climb seems to last forever in the gloom of the tunnel. But eventually the gloom starts to clear, and you fancy you can see light ahead. Sure enough, the gradient of the tunnel starts to level out and the air gets clearer.

Then you are at the top. Above you is a long, tall ladder, bolted to a short, round, stone clad tunnel rising upwards like a chimney, and on top of this you can just see a metal grate. Light spills down through the gaps in the grate. The night is giving way to dawn, and never have you been so glad to see the suns in the sky above.

You start the long climb up the ladder and reach the top, breathing heavily, and try to open the grate. It is locked. Do you have the **SKILL OF LOCK PICKING**. If you do turn to **40**

If you do not, you will have to try to burn through the metal. You remember you have some corrosives in glass vials. You take them out and remove the glass stopper. Then you reach through and pour the acid into the lock. **TEST YOUR FORTUNE.** If you pass, turn to **40**. If you fail, turn the page and read on……..

Despite your best efforts, the lock on the grate remains. The acid seems to have little effect on the metal and just drops down and burns your arms. Lose **2 ENDURANCE** points. You try to shake the grate free, but it's useless.

You realise with no way out of here, you will have to try to return to the chamber and avoid De-Villiers spectral form. You climb back down the ladder and start to descend back down to the chamber.

You are about halfway down when you feel a rumbling in the ground, as if many footsteps were running up the tunnel. Something is heading back up the tunnel as you walk down it. You are just realising this when you turn a corner.

Ahead of you is an army of skeletons, each armed with short swords and shields. They swarm up the tunnel, some seeming to run along the sides of the walls and the ceilings. Then they are on you. You try to fight, but there are too many, and they swarm over you, their short swords stabbing and cutting. You are cut into bloody rags in moments.

You were so close to escaping, but sadly your promising career as a thief has been cut short.

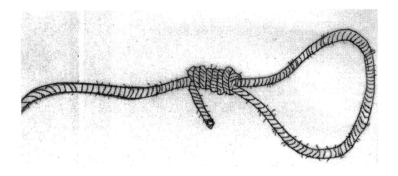

# BONUS ADVENTURE

# THE LABYRINTHS OF LAEVENI

## PART ONE

Beneath the ancient city of Laeveni, unknown to the majority of the population, lies a set of tunnels and catacombs. The cold, dark stone corridors and rooms predate even the earliest buildings in Laeveni.  Locked inside these labyrinths are some of the foulest creatures ever to have lived – who survive by feeding off the weak.

You find yourself sentenced to a crime of heresy and as punishment you have been thrown into the labyrinth with no weapons and no food. All you can do is try to survive and escape.

# LABYRINTH 1

**COMBAT** is by rolling 2d6 and adding it to your **FIGHTING SKILL**. Do the same for your opponent. Whomever has the highest total wins that round. The loser is injured and loses 2 **ENDURANCE** points. Keep rolling until one of you ends up at 0 **ENDURANCE** – and is dead.

Each time you enter a new room (a new section number) you have to roll 2d6 and consult the Labyrinth Chart for this Labyrinth.

If you roll a number that has an X underneath it, the room is empty, return to the reference you were on, and choose a new direction.

If you roll a number that has a reference number below, then turn to that reference and follow the instructions. But note down which reference you are on – as you will return there (if you survive!).

The sections are numbered to fit in with a larger book that will be hopefully released at some stage – but this adventure starts rather traditionally at reference **1**.

# 1

Each time you enter a new room, unless told otherwise, roll 2d6 and consult Labyrinth Chart A below:

## LABYRINTH CHART A

| 2 | 3 | 4 | 5 | 6 | 7 | 8 | 9 | 10 | 11 | 12 |
|---|---|---|---|---|---|---|---|----|----|----|
| 81 | X | 66 | 60 | X | 243 | 96 | 138 | 217 | X | 108 |

If you roll **X**, then you enter an empty room or area and you progress without incident. If you roll a number with a reference, note the current reference you are on and turn to the new reference.

You may want to copy the Labyrinth chart onto a separate piece of paper to safe constantly turning back to this page.

Now you have to try to survive the first labyrinth and find what you need to escape it.

All in darkness, the door slams shut behind you. You try it – locked and solid metal. With the door locked behind you, you have no option but to go straight on.

Turn to **235**

# 11

Roll 2d6 and consult Labyrinth Chart A
**Rolled X or returning**

On the wall straight ahead of you is a small window barred with a thick iron grill. A faint light shines through it but it's too high up in the wall for you to see anything out of it.

You can now:
Head left, turn to **117**
To turn right, turn to **230**
Go back the way you came, turn to **197**

# 17
Roll 2d6 and consult Labyrinth Chart A
**Rolled X or returning**

Leaving the skeletal remains behind, you walk up a short incline up into a new room. On the wall on the left there is a small window barred with thick iron bars. A faint light shines through it but it's too high up in the wall for you to see anything out of it.

What will you do?
Go right, turn to **197**
To go back the way you came, turn to **117**
Go straight on, turn to **230**

# 18
Roll 2d6 and consult Labyrinth Chart A
**Rolled X or returning**

You appear to be at a T-junction. Straight ahead is a stone wall. Hanging from it in manacles is a skeleton. The bones are yellowed with age and what was once its clothing hang off it in rags.

You can only choose to turn left or right, or if you would prefer you can go back the way you came. The left passage seems to go downhill and seems even darker and murkier.

The right passage climbs up slightly, and there seems to be a slight glow of light at the end before the corridor bends out of sight

You can now:
Go left, turn to **46**
Go straight on, turn to **17**
Return the way you came, turn to **38**

## 29

Roll 2d6 and consult Labyrinth Chart A
**Rolled X or returning**

You walk into a small, round room. The only exit is to your left.

To go left, turn to **113**
To head back the way you came, turn to **178**

## 38

Roll 2d6 and consult Labyrinth Chart A
**Rolled X or returning**

There is only one way out of this room, a turning to the left.

Your choices are now:
Go left, turn to **239**
Head back the way you came, turn to **18**

## 41

Roll 2d6 and consult Labyrinth Chart A
**Rolled X or returning**

You enter a small, round room. There is only one exit, a turning to the right

To go right, turn to **178**
To go back around the curved corridor, turn to **113**

## 46

Roll 2d6 and consult Labyrinth Chart A
**Rolled X or returning**

The corridor goes downhill and soon; earth replaces the flagstones under your feet. The temperature increases and the air is increasingly musty. Soon you come to a doorway.
Your options are simple:

To go back the way you came, turn to **236**
Go through the doorway, turn to **56**

## 56

Roll 2d6 and consult Labyrinth Chart A
**Rolled X or returning**

Opening the door carefully, you slip through it into a simple chamber. There is a table and a few chairs in the corner. It seems like it's some sort of guard room.

Your options are now:
Go right, turn to **224**
To go back the way you came, turn to **109**

## 60

On the floor you notice a parcel. You pick it up warily and open it – the smell of fresh bread hits your nostrils. Grateful, you wolf down the food.

Gain **1 ENDURANCE** point. If you roll **5** again in this reference, class it as an X roll for the remainder of this labyrinth.

Turn back to your previous reference.

## 65

Roll 2d6 and consult Labyrinth Chart A
**Rolled X or returning**

You head back into the guardroom to try to find the key that will let you escape this labyrinth.

If you now have a small brass key, then return to **224**
Otherwise the only way you can go is to the left, turn to **109**

## 66

You creep into the next location and are aware of a shuffling figure ahead of you. Its short, only about 4-foot-tall, but it hisses and leaps at you without warning. You must fight it

**KOBOLD    FS 4    ENDURANCE 6**

If you win, any **ENDURANCE** you have lost will return by **1 POINT** for each X roll.
Now turn back to your previous reference.

## 73

Roll 2d6 and consult Labyrinth Chart A
**Rolled X or returning**

The wall extends into the distance on your left hand side and there appears to be no gaps in it. You feel your way along the wall and then come to a dead end ahead of you. To your right there is a low archway. You options now are to:
Go back the way you came, turn to **239**
Duck through the doorway to the right, turn to **18**

# KOBOLD

**FIGHTING SKILL**: 4          **ENDURANCE**: 6

**MONSTER TYPE**: Minion

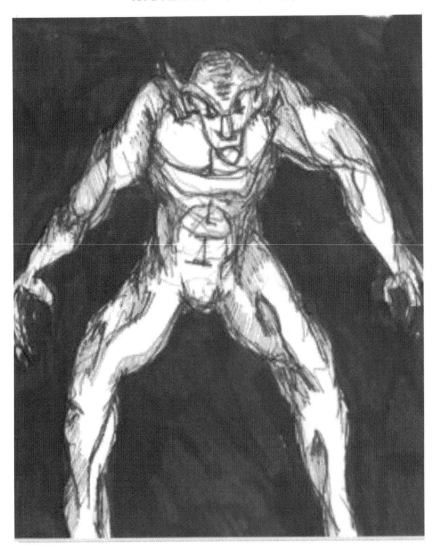

# 74

Roll 2d6 and consult Labyrinth Chart A
**Rolled X or returning**

The room in a hexagonal chamber with a dark alter raised up opposite you. Behind the altar is a huge statue of some sort of Daemon. The statue is fully 12 feet high and seems to emanate pure evil.

**TEST YOUR FORTUNE**

To do this, roll 2d6 and note the score. Then roll 2d6 again. If the first number is higher, then turn to **147**

If it is lower or equal to the second score, turn to **154**

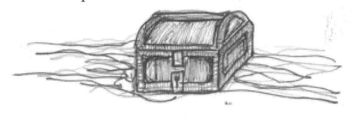

# 81

As you enter this area, your foot catches on something. You bend down and see a glint of metal. Carefully, in case it's a trap, you move the dirt from around the metallic object to reveal the hilt of a sword. You pull it free and shake the dust off it. Despite the muck and cobwebs on it, the steel is still sound. Add 2 to your **FIGHTING SKILL**

If you roll 2 again in this labyrinth, class it as an X roll.

Turn to your previous reference

You pull the small brass key form your tunic pocket, and put in in the lock and turn. There is a "*click*" and you pull on the handle. The door swings open. You have escaped the first labyrinth.

If you wish to use this as a save point, record your current attributes and remember if you die to start again from this reference.

You exit the labyrinth. The door swings closed behind you. In front of you is a set of stairs leading to an archway.

## THE END OF LABYRINTH ONE

## TURN TO ?

## PART TWO OF

# THE LABYRINTHS OF LAEVENI

## IS AVAILABLE AS THE BONUS ADVENTURE IN:

### Shadow Thief Book 2: Hunted

### Available from August 2020

# ORC FOOT SOLDIER

**FIGHTING SKILL:** 5　　　　　　　**ENDURANCE:** 8

**MONSTER TYPE:** Underling

## 96

You walk into this new area and find that in front of you is an orc foot soldier. Given their excellent night vision, he has already seen you and moves to attack. You must fight

**ORC FOOT SOLDIER      FS 5      ENDURANCE 8**

If you win, gain **1 FIGHTING SKILL** and any **ENDURANCE** you have lost will return by **1 POINT** for each X roll. If you roll **8** in this labyrinth again, class it as an X roll.
Now turn back to your previous reference.

## 108

You walk into the darkened area but then you feel a sudden pain in the small of your back, and look down in surprise to see a rusty iron blade protruding from under your rib cage. The blade is slick with your blood. An Orc Captain, who has sneaked up on you in surprise, pulls the blade downwards into your innards.
You die in torment.

## 109

Roll 2d6 and consult Labyrinth Chart A
**Rolled X or returning**
Leaving the guardroom, you are back in the corridor which now leads uphill.
You have few choices. You can:
Return to the guardroom and turn to **56**
Go straight on up the corridor and turn to **236**

## 113

Roll 2d6 and consult Labyrinth Chart A

**Rolled X or returning**

The curved corridor takes you into another room with two
exits. You can either:
Go left, turn to **210**
To go back the way you came along the curved corridor, turn
to **41**
Go straight on, turn to **74**

# 117

Roll 2d6 and consult Labyrinth Chart A
**Rolled X or returning**

Having chance to look around the room, you see on your right
is a skeleton hanging from the walls by rusted old manacles.
The bones are yellowed with age and what was once its
clothing hang off it in rags.
Your choices are:
To go left, turn to **38**
To go back the way you came, turn to **17**
Go straight on, turn to **46**

# ORC CAPTAIN

**FIGHTING SKILL:** 6            **ENDURANCE:** 10

**MONSTER TYPE**: Boss

# 138

You walk into this new area and find that in front of you is an orc captain. Given their excellent night vision, he has already seen you and moves to attack.  You must fight

**ORC CAPTAIN**          **FS 6    ENDURANCE 10**

If you win, gain **1 FIGHTING SKILL.** If you roll **9** again, class it as an X role. Turn to **143**

# 143

You search the hideous creature's tunic and find a small brass key. This is the key out of this labyrinth. You now just need to find the door.

If you roll **10** again in this labyrinth, class it as an X roll. Now return to the reference you were on before fighting the orc captain.

# 147

You feel the evil presence in the statue reaching out towards you. You try to turn and run, but you are rooted to the spot, unable to move a muscle. You feel the touch of an alien mind on yours – a gentle almost caressing touch. Then you manage to compose yourself and turn and run from the evil room.

Turn to **174**

# 154

You feel the evil presence in the statue reaching out towards you. You try to turn and run, but you are rooted to the spot, unable to move a muscle. You feel the touch of an alien mind on yours – a gentle almost caressing touch. But then the caress turns into an assault and the mind overwhelms your consciousness and you feel your sanity slipping away.

You are left a gibbering wreck or a person, stripped of reason, and doomed to roam the halls of this labyrinth until you die.

## 174

Roll 2d6 and consult Labyrinth Chart A
**Rolled X or returning**
You leave the dread temple and are back in a normal room. You can now:
Go right, turn to **210**
Go straight on, turn to **41**

## 178

Roll 2d6 and consult Labyrinth Chart A
**Rolled X or returning**

You recognise the room you enter straight away. On your left is the locked steel door that you came in through. You try it one again, just in case it is now unlocked, but to no avail.

Your options are:
To head right, turn to **11**
To go back the way you came, turn to **29**
Go straight on, turn to **73**

# 197

Roll 2d6 and consult Labyrinth Chart A
**Rolled X or returning**

Straight ahead of you is the large metal door you came in by. You are back where you started. You curse under your breath.

Looking around the room, you see that you can either:
Go left, turn to **29**
To go back the way you came, turn to **11**
To turn right, turn to **73**

# 210

Roll 2d6 and consult Labyrinth Chart A
**Rolled X or returning**

On the wall to your right is a small window barred with a thick iron grill. A faint light shines through it but it's too high up in the wall for you to see anything out of it.

Your options are now:
Go left, turn to **197**
To go back the way you came, turn to **230**
Go straight on, turn to **117**

## 217

As you place your foot down, you hear a "*tek*" and then you feel a stabbing pain in your ankle. You look down and see that you have stepped into a bear trap. You pull the jaws open and manage to release your foot. Fortunately, the thick leather of your boot has caught most of the damage. You limp off, ensuring the trap is closed in case you come this way again.

Lose 1 **ENDURANCE** point

If you roll **10** again in this reference, class it as an X roll for the remainder of this labyrinth.

Turn back to your previous reference.

## 224

Roll 2d6 and consult Labyrinth Chart A
**Rolled X or returning**

This room is dominated by a large brass door at the end of it. In the centre is a doorknob and to its right is a small keyhole. You try the doorknob and the door is, unsurprisingly, locked

If you have a small brass key, turn to **88**
If you don't, you will have to go back the way you came, turn to **65**

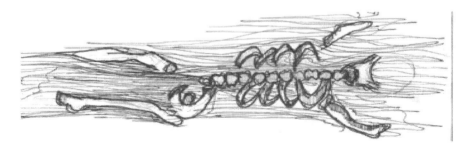

## 230

Roll 2d6 and consult Labyrinth Chart A
**Rolled X or returning**

You arrive in a room with two exits. One is to the left, the other to the right is a curved corridor.

If you choose to turn left, turn to **74**
To go back the way you came, turn to **210**
To go right down the curved corridor, turn to **41**

## 235

The room in front of you in dark and smells of dirt and decay. There are no torches on the wall and no natural light and so all you can see is gloom. You can hear voices, growls and groans, but they seem to echo off the walls and so you have no idea if they are close or distant.

Roll 2d6 and consult Labyrinth Chart A. If the number you roll corresponds to an X, then go straight to the bold text blow. If you need to turn to another reference on Chart A, then make a note of this section, and if you survive what you encounter in the new section, then return here and read on:

**Rolled X or returning**
You cannot see for more than a few feet in any direction, but you can make out that there are three doorways leading out of this room. You can choose to:
Go left, turn to **73**
Go straight on, turn to **11**
Go right, turn to **29**

## 236

Roll 2d6 and consult Labyrinth Chart A
**Rolled X or returning**

You walk back up the corridor, breathing heavily due to the gradient of the passage. Soon the earth turns back to flagstones and you are back in a room. On your left is a skeleton hanging from the walls by rusted old manacles. The bones are yellowed with age and what was once its clothing hang off it in rags.

You can:
Go right, turn to **38**
To go back the way you came, turn to **46**
Go straight on, turn to **17**

## 239

Roll 2d6 and consult Labyrinth Chart A
**Rolled X or returning**

You are back where you started, with the large metal door to your right.
Your options are:
Go left, turn to **11**
Go straight on, turn to **29**

## 243

On the floor you notice a bottle. You pick it up warily and open it – it smells invigorating. You drain the bottle and feel stronger. You have drunk a potion of **SKILL**.

Gain **1 FIGHTING SKILL**. If you roll **7** again in this reference, class it as an X roll for the remainder of this labyrinth.

Turn back to your previous reference.

Other gamebooks from

# BLACK DOG GAMEBOOKS

## AVAILABLE NOW:
*The Hellscape Book 1:*
*Straight to Hell*

## COMING SOON:

*Shadow Thief Book 2: Hunted (August 2020)*

Psycho Killer
(October 2020)

*The Hellscape Book 2:*
*The Devils Right Hand (est 2021)*

*Shadow Thief Book 3 (est 2021)*